'[...] ...nt

...and future YA stars. [...] by turns heart-warming, thought-provoking and unsettling, *A Change Is Gonna Come* has something for everyone. I highly recommend this book.'
Cat Clarke, author of *Girlhood*

'This is an essential collection for young people, and all readers who feel other, to realize they are not alone.'
Sarah Shaffi, Online Editor and Producer at *The Bookseller*, and books previewer at *Stylist*

'[...] an inspirational collection of voices – all of which are bound by the same energy and vigour, the same desire to bring about something new.'
Pooja Puri, author of *The Jungle*

'This lyrical and timely collection offers readers mirrors to feel a sense of belonging and opens a wider window on to a world of stories and storytellers who are writing the change.'
Sita Brahmachari, author of *Tender Earth*

'[A C... ...is summer.'

STRIPES PUBLISHING
An imprint of the Little Tiger Group
1 Coda Studios, 189 Munster Road, London SW6 6AW

A paperback original
First published in Great Britain in 2017

ISBN: 978-1-84715-839-0

A CIP catalogue record for this book is available from the British Library.

Printed and bound in the UK.

2 4 6 8 10 9 7 5 3

A CHANGE IS GONNA COME

MARY BELLO • AISHA BUSHBY • TANYA BYRNE
INUA ELLAMS • CATHERINE JOHNSON
PATRICE LAWRENCE • AYISHA MALIK • IRFAN MASTER
MUSA OKWONGA • YASMIN RAHMAN
PHOEBE ROY • NIKESH SHUKLA

stripes

A Note on the Stories

The purpose of this anthology is to give creative space to those who have historically had their thoughts, ideas and experiences oppressed. As such, we have not censored the topics covered by our writers. If you're worried about coming across something that is particularly upsetting to you, see page 320 for the list of topics covered. We have included some resources that might help if you are affected by any of the issues raised or would like to find out more.

Contents

Foreword

I was delighted to be asked to write a foreword to this book. It features some of my favourite authors, as well as authors I strongly suspect will become new favourites. 'A Change Is Gonna Come' is, as you probably know, the title of a song written by Sam Cooke that became an anthem of the 1960s Civil Rights struggle in the USA. It's a song that captures the pain of racial injustice but also the determination and optimism required to change things for the better.

Some changes are inevitable – night and day; the seasons; birth, ageing and death. Some proverbs – 'You can't teach an old dog new tricks', 'A leopard never changes its spots' – suggest that change is impossible. But many changes are neither inevitable nor impossible. That's what makes 'change' such a fascinating topic.

The tension between changing to 'fit into' the world and changing the world to be more like we want it to be is present in so much storytelling. We can think of change as the space between who we are and who we want to be – between being and becoming – as individuals and as communities. Change is not inevitable or impossible; it requires imagination to picture how things might be, as well as courage and tenacity to work to make the imagined a reality.

As a teacher, I want those I teach to believe that the stories they write can be about people like them. Yet many don't, and indeed one child in my class announced that he thought 'stories have to be about white people'. I think children's writing often imitates their reading and there is plenty of evidence available that the range of books for children and young people being published is still too narrow and doesn't reflect the country or the world in which we live. But, although it's been a long time coming, this is beginning to change.

Writers, like teachers, need to have optimistic views on change. You could say that both are in the business of 'changing minds' in some sense – not just their own minds but also the minds of other people. 'A Change Is Gonna Come' is no mere prediction. It's an expression of hope and intent. As James Baldwin wrote, 'Not everything that is faced can be changed, but nothing can be changed until it is faced.'

Thank you to Stripes for facing the situation in children's publishing. Thank you to the writers in this book for their imagination, their optimism and their determination. May we all be inspired, emboldened and yes, changed, by reading their words.

Darren Chetty – May 2017

Introduction

A Change Is Gonna Come has developed from a determination to convert hope into action, desire into intention. We know there is a wealth of talented writers of colour out there and we know their voices aren't reaching readers as often as they should. Each of the twelve writers in this collection has brought their own individual take on the theme of 'change'. The stories are inspiring but not all of them are stories of success and I wouldn't have it any other way.

As Musa Okwonga's poem, 'The Elders on the Wall' expresses, change is difficult, not least for those who are leading the way. The second poem in the collection, Inua Ellams's 'Of Lizard Skin and Dust Storms', encapsulates the inescapable tension between change as both loss and gain.

The stories gathered in this book take the reader from a past filled with prejudice and bravery of spirit, as in Catherine Johnson's 'Astounding Talent! Unequalled Performances!' to a future where prejudice still exists but spirit has not been extinguished either, in Patrice

Lawrence's story 'The Clean Sweep'. In both, it is clear that the people we love are central to everything.

First love is the focus of Tanya Byrne's 'Hackney Moon', a vision of hope for what is possible that should be held close at heart by anyone who has felt lost; Irfan Master, by contrast, reaches for the seemingly impossible in a mind-bending journey through time. The anchor, of course, is love.

None of the writers here are afraid of taking on big questions, of looking at the world we live in and asking us to think a little harder and a little deeper at why things are the way they are. Why don't things change? Why can't they? Nikesh Shukla's 'We Who?' and Ayisha Malik's 'A Refuge' both take up this cry.

And as change is, without doubt, about the future, I must make special mention of the four new voices included in the collection. Talented writers who are just at the beginning of their writing careers and whose names I am sure you will see adorning the covers of novels and story collections of the future. The publishing industry is changing and the incredible writing produced here is evidence of that. Discover a world where the mythic and the everyday intertwine in Phoebe Roy's 'Iridescent Adolescent', glimpse the struggle of a girl trying desperately to maintain control in Aisha Bushby's 'Marionette Girl', share in the sadness of losing someone and the joy of gaining unexpected new friendships in Mary Bello's 'Dear Asha' and see what impact a chance encounter can have in Yasmin Rahman's 'Fortune Favours the Bold'. I, for one, cannot wait to read more from each of these talented writers.

May the writing in this book be an inspiration and a statement of fact: a change is gonna come.

Ruth Bennett, Editorial Director
Stripes Publishing – May 2017

Working on this anthology has been an incredible experience. Not only does it represent an important step forwards, it also showcases outstanding talent. Every teen deserves to be their own protagonist and at long last here is a book to reflect that.

Aa'Ishah Z. Hawton
A Change Is Gonna Come Editorial Mentee

THE ELDERS ON THE WALL

·

Musa Okwonga

I wish to change the world, and the elders smirk
Since all I see before me is this:
Their thousand-mile-high wall
With no visible places to grip.
Even if I climb it,
I'll have to leave so many behind
While I rise towards these elders, who yell
That they made it up there without help.
"You youths can reach where we are if you toil,"
They say, pouring oil down that wall's face.
They didn't build this edifice,
But they don't seem aggrieved that it's complete.
What to do? The wall extends
In either direction and out of view.
My choices are two:
Either I stand here,
Chip away at each brick,
Or, more dangerously, turn and run from the crowd
Till I no longer hear their anguished shouts,
And somehow tumble forwards over those roughest roads,
Those loneliest hills, and sprint, convinced
There's better out there, for all of us.
I run, raging and so afraid,

Joyfully and terrifyingly uncaged,
To lands that even maps dare not touch,
Through thoughts that scream I'll not amount to much,
Through dry-throated mornings, tears of regret,
Fevers of loneliness, migraines of lost faith;
And all that time, there's no cloak
Round my shoulders, no warm arm, because all
Of those I love are chipping at that wall,
Wishing for its fall.
I lurch on, beyond self-doubt,
Then further still, till I black out –
And find myself atop a cloud,
Looking down towards that wall,
Behind which the elders are scurrying and scared.
I call, though unsure I may be heard:
"Change is hard; still, maintain the charge.
They may have the safety,
But the bravery is all ours."
I fear my message may not have drifted down
Since the wind up here is strong,
But then a friend raises a hand to hail me,
And they press on.

MARIONETTE GIRL

·

Aisha Bushby

Ask me anything about Harry Potter. Seriously. I've done twenty-three quizzes online so far and got one hundred per cent on all of them. I'm a Gryffindor, apparently, although I don't feel brave most of the time. Usually I feel scared when things don't go to plan, but that's for another conversation.

My wand is seven inches, maple, unicorn hair, bendy.

The bit about the unicorn hair is my favourite.

Maple is supposed to mean I'm a natural traveller and adventurer. That made me laugh. On a scale of adventurousness, I don't even register.

Oh, and my patronus is a cat. That I can believe because cats thrive on routine. Did you know that if you try and disrupt their routine it messes with their mental health?

I did, because I've researched it.

A lot.

FRIDAY
12.01 p.m.

Maths is my favourite subject. I like the certainty of it. We spend the first half of the lesson learning a new formula and the second half applying it to a worksheet. Also, unlike in English, we aren't asked to contribute our opinions. That terrifies me.

But today is different.

I go to sit at my usual spot: third row in, by the wall. I don't sit right at the back where Callum and his minions cluster, nor do I sit at the front.

But today someone else has taken my seat and I freeze, actually freeze, by the door when I see her. A few people who had been following behind bump into my heavy rucksack and swear at me, but I don't care. Eventually they squeeze past while I stay glued to the spot.

"A problem, Amani?" Mr Delacourt asks. He has a stern-looking face with a thick greying moustache and he always sounds sarcastic, even when he's being sincere.

"Um…" I pause. I want to say someone is in my place but it's a girl who's just visiting for the day before deciding whether to join our school next year. Milly Wilkinson. Our form tutor, Ms Yates, introduced her to us this morning and she looks terrified.

Plus it's petty, isn't it?

Even so, I hope this doesn't mean I'll have to move around during my other lessons. Mr Delacourt's drawl interrupts my worries.

"Well, then, take your seat," he says, shuffling through his papers. Everyone is starting to stare. I take the only seat left, which is right in front of Mr Delacourt's desk, and already I feel exposed.

I drop my bag to the floor, sit down and pull the chair forwards. As I do I feel something pliable beneath my fingers. I cringe. Someone has stuck a piece of used gum under the chair and I've just touched it.

My uncontaminated hand shoots up.

"Yes, Amani?" Mr Delacourt sighs.

"Please may I go to the toilet?" I ask. *Please, please, please.* My heart beats in time with the request. I can feel the germs dancing across my fingers – it makes them tingle.

"Has someone put you up to this?" He sounds irritated now.

"What? No, I—"

"You had plenty of time to go to the toilet during break. I'm sure you can hold it until lunch." Without a pause he launches into the lesson, but I can't concentrate.

All I can think about is washing my hands. I can't touch any of my things, either, so I flip through my book one-handed.

Mr Delacourt's words float in one ear and out the other. My mind is too full of worries to absorb anything.

Instead I sit and watch as the clock tick-tocks closer to 1.00 p.m.

1.03 p.m.

I'm in the girls' toilets before most people have even made it out of their lessons. I let the tap run extra hot and stick my hand under it for as long as I can bear.

I feel the anxiety slip down the drain as I wash.

But once isn't enough.

One, two, three.

Some girls walk in and I have to speed up my ritual.

They can't know.

1.27 p.m.

"Chicken and sweetcorn again?" Gabby teases.

I look up from my lunch in time to catch the amused expression on her face.

"And, let me guess." Efe joins us at the table. "Salt and vinegar crisps?" She grins. "And…"

"A Mars bar!" they both finish together in a fit of giggles.

"You are a weird one, Amani," Gabby says, smiling at me fondly.

Whenever we get into this sort of territory, I clam up. "Ha, yeah," I mumble, swallowing half of my sandwich in one go. It hurts as it goes down – too dry.

But they've already moved on to discussing their summer plans, barely registering as I sink further into myself.

They don't mean to be unkind.

They just don't understand.

3.45 p.m.

The bell rings, signalling the end of the day, and I rush out to meet Dad, who should be waiting in the car park.

Or, at least, I try.

On the way out Callum intercepts me. "Hey, Am-aaar-niii," he says, standing in my way.

I hate the way he stresses the vowels in my name, drawing them out. He always likes to point out how 'foreign' my name is.

Callum's the popular guy at school and he loves to exercise his power by getting a few laughs from his friends. Unfortunately tormenting people like me will do it.

I don't say anything, just keep my head down and try to push past. We do a little dance as he matches his steps to mine.

Eventually I mumble a request for him to move.

"What was that?" he asks exaggeratedly.

I glance at the clock. 3.51 p.m. I'm officially late. We won't make it home in time.

Callum still doesn't move and my hands start

shaking. I know he's taunting me but all I can hear is the blood pulsing in my ears as the clock ticks on and on.

Eventually I shove him aside, adrenaline fuelling me. I hear him yell after me, "Oi, you bit—" but I'm already out of the door before I can hear the rest, my breath coming in heavy pants as I race to Dad's car.

I'll pay for this on Monday but right now I don't care.

"We have to hurry!" I cry as soon as I get in.

"Well, hello to you, too," Dad remarks, but he starts the car quickly after he sees my face.

"How much time do we have?"

"Five minutes," I say, glancing at the clock.

"Don't worry," Dad says, determined. "We'll make it in time."

I wonder what would happen if we didn't make it in time. I don't find out as Dad speeds to get home and we step through the front door at 3.59 p.m. I know this because I set an alarm to go off at 4.00 p.m. It vibrates in my pocket just as I rush up the stairs to my room.

As I step inside I feel my chest deflate, the tension oozing out of my body.

I have several alarms that get me through the day.

This is one of them.

It's hard to explain why I do this. But try to imagine that your brain is going to internally combust unless you walk through the door of your home before 4.00 p.m.

And then ask yourself what you would do if you were in my shoes.

SATURDAY
7.23 a.m.

My alarm wakes me up. The first thing I do is check to see if I have any notifications on my phone. Sometimes it takes the whole seven minutes, other times it doesn't. Today is one of those days where I'm done by 7.26 a.m.

I can't get up though – not until 7.30 a.m. It's kind of like the floor is lava, except the lava is inside my stomach. I can't leave my room until 8.00 a.m., either. It seems odd but I didn't decide these rules – my brain did.

I just follow them.

Even though it's the weekend I won't sleep in –

I don't remember the last time I did.

It's never as bad when I'm at school. There's a timetable and I stick to it. Then the evenings usually go: homework, teatime, TV, read and bed.

It's the weekends I find hard.

Dad always suggests days out but the idea of not getting back in time scares me a little too much and I usually ignore him. (See, I'm definitely not a Gryffindor and my wand isn't maple). Mum understands my routine and we work around it together. But she's not here today.

I spend the next few minutes peering out of the window from my bed. All I can see is a cloudless sky and the tops of the trees as they rustle in the breeze. It's sunny today and the light is shining through my blinds in delicate strands. I watch the little dust particles float in the air in front of me. They sway to and fro, and for a while it's like nothing else exists in the world.

It's a relief not to think about anything for a minute, until I hear Dad start the blender. He's making one of his gross breakfast smoothies again. The sound puts me on edge and reality comes crashing back into my mind.

He finishes by 7.29 a.m. and it feels like I can

breathe again.

Then, my second alarm of the day goes off.

7.30 a.m.

Hermione is sleeping on the teal chair that sits in one corner of my room. It has this fringing on each of the arms that she loves, and she spends ages playing with it.

If you're confused, Hermione is my cat.

She's a really pretty tortoiseshell and she hates feet. If you put even a toe near her she'll growl at you and cat-walk away. We get along because she's just as set in her ways as I am.

Every night when I go to bed I leave the door open just a little and every morning when I wake up, she's there, sleeping.

I stroke her three times before I go for a shower. I don't know what I'd do if the bathroom wasn't connected to my room.

I won't tell you about this bit of my routine because that's, well, kind of weird.

When I'm back I stroke her two times and get ready for the day. I always lay out my clothes the night before. They're folded neatly at the end of my bed. I dress slowly and even then I'm done by 7.51 a.m.

I stroke Hermione, just once this time, and that's usually when Dad calls for me, even though we both know I'll be down at 8.00 a.m.

Dad works from home doing design stuff, so we have breakfast together on Saturdays before he finishes his jobs for the week. Mum's usually still asleep but today she's at some sort of academic conference.

I wait at the threshold of my room, one hand poised on the doorknob, the other flicking through my phone, until the alarm goes off.

As I mentioned, I have all these alarms on my phone to remind me what I have to do next. It keeps me motivated.

I tap off the alarm and, before I leave, I take a last look at Hermione through the doorway.

She'll be in there for a few more hours.

8.00 a.m.

This is when it gets a little more difficult.

Outside my room there are all these external factors

that I can't control and just the thought of it is making my mouth go dry.

Especially after yesterday.

"Hey, Dad," I say as I sit at my usual spot at the dining table.

"Yo," Dad says, barely looking up from his paper. It's either his attempt at a joke or sounding cool, I can't really tell which.

I give him a grudging smile and take a sip of tea. I have this mug that says 'Don't Let the Muggles Get You Down' and it's my favourite.

It's not that Dad and I don't get along. I love him, of course. It's that he doesn't always understand my issues. I once heard him say to Mum that if they left me to it, I'd 'snap out of it'. He didn't exactly say I was attention-seeking, but it was definitely implied.

Dad looks up and frowns. "Your hands are a little dry today." That's all he says.

Dad'll never properly engage me in a conversation about it. Mum will always ask directly: "Amani, have you been washing your hands again?" Sounds like a strange question, doesn't it? I mean, most parents would be pleased to have a hygienic child. But there's that and then there's using a whole bottle of handwash a day.

That's not normal.

They tried to send me to a therapist once. His advice was that I should have an allocated budget for cleaning products each week. The idea was that I would learn to ration myself, like we're in some sort of zombie apocalypse. But that didn't work. Four days in and I'd already used all of the money, and had to beg Mum for more. It got so bad I was on the floor screaming, just screaming at her. She cried. I cried. Dad walked out of the house and didn't come back all evening.

We stopped going after that.

The kitchen smells like fresh coffee and toast today, and that's when I notice the problem.

"Dad?" He doesn't answer. I clear my throat. "Dad, why aren't we having eggy bread?"

Every Saturday we have eggy bread. That's how it is.

I stare at the pile of toast and spreads teasing me from the centre of the table.

Dad sighs deeply, like the world's problems are lodged in his oesophagus. "We ran out of eggs," he says simply, staring me down.

It's a challenge.

My palms start sweating and it's as if my chest is on fire. I can feel the tears coming on. That makes me sound like a brat, doesn't it? Crying over eggy bread. But it's not like that, I swear.

I grip the edge of the table and stare down at the empty plate. Dad is still looking at me, I can tell. And then I bolt, right out of the room and back upstairs. I get under the bedcovers and I cry.

I cry because I can't eat the toast. I cry because I'm stuck in a time warp – one where I'm doomed to live the same day over and over again and there's nothing I can do about it. I cry because Dad doesn't understand.

Eventually, when I can't cry any more, I sit up. My pillow is wet and scrunched up but I place it roughly behind my back. I look over at my chair for Hermione but she's gone.

12.51 p.m.

Dad's gone out, so it's just me. That helps. It means I can get on with my day without worrying about someone else's movements. He didn't check on me, even though I was crying loud enough to make the walls shake. It's like he's scared of me, like I have some sort of contagious disease.

When I go downstairs there's a note to say a new printer is going to be delivered between 9.00 a.m. and 6.00 p.m. I hate that it's such a big window. I feel I have to sit and wait the whole time, on edge for when the doorbell rings. The best thing to do, I decide, is to start a new book from my never-ending pile and read until the delivery arrives.

I'm enjoying the book. It's about a girl who's mixed race, like me, who has anxiety, like me. Her dad dies and she can't cope. She's taken to a fantasy world where she has to fight a demon. I'm only a third of the way in but things aren't going too well for her right now. I can relate.

1.47 p.m.

The doorbell rings and Dad's still not home. But when I answer it, it isn't the delivery. It's my aunt. She sometimes likes to just 'pop round' for a cup of tea. She hasn't quite mastered the art of texting or calling beforehand. Her impromptu visits make me nervous, especially as she has this way of talking *at* you, not *with* you.

"Amani, how lovely to see you," she says, her voice flat. "Is your dad around?" she asks, glancing past me, no doubt hoping he might materialize.

"Um, no…" I say, shuffling my feet.

"Ah, right, of course," she says, as if she knew this already. "Well?" She's still hovering. I'm hoping she'll leave. "Let me in for a cuppa, will you?" she finally asks, bustling past me. "I'll just wait until he gets back."

I'm still facing the door, which is good because that means she can't see the face I just pulled. I take a few deep breaths before looking up and there's the delivery man, staring down at me.

"Hello, love," he says, a little too cheerfully. "Sign here, please. Can I just have…"

I don't hear what he says next because my aunt is making a lot of noise behind me, clattering through the cupboards.

"Am, where's the Earl Grey?" she asks.

I cringe. I hate that nickname.

At exactly the same moment, the man holds out this

machine to get my electronic signature. I can't handle the two things happening at once so I cover my ears with my hands.

"Oh, for goodness' sake," my aunt scolds, walking to the door. "Thank you," she says to the man, giving me side-eye while she smiles at him.

"Are you OK?" he asks, looking between me and my aunt as she takes the box. It's clear he's jumping to all sorts of conclusions, so I smile.

"Fine," I say.

"Here it is!" she sings from the kitchen as she turns on the kettle.

The man frowns down at me but nods, before stepping away.

"Thank you," I add, for good measure.

Back in the kitchen my aunt rounds on me. "Honestly, Amani, you're not a child. You need to learn to do these sorts of things without help. What would you've done if I wasn't here? What'll you do when you're off to uni?" She stares down at me and I don't have the energy to explain that I probably won't be going to university because of my illness. So instead, I busy myself setting up the printer while she sits with her tea.

She hasn't taken off her shoes and I'm imagining all the germs on the carpet. I can see this path where's she stepped, like a slug trail. I imagine my aunt as a giant slug for a moment and it makes me feel a little better.

2.33 p.m.

Dad's home. It turns out he was running some errands, including a food shop, and I know it was to buy me eggs. I barricade myself in my room. I can hear my aunt talk about me from up here, her voice penetrating the walls. I can hear Dad, too, though he speaks too quietly for me to know what he's saying. His voice sounds annoyed but I'm not sure if it's aimed at me or her.

I'm still reading my book. I've decided I'm going to spend the rest of my day reading because leaving my room is too stressful. Dad knocks on my door and the sound sends jolts of anxiety through my body.

"Amani?" he calls, his voice muffled.

"Come in," I say, my voice hoarse.

"She's gone now." He grins sheepishly. "She's a bit full-on, isn't she?" he says.

I nod. I can't explain that for me it's more than that.

"Want some lunch? You haven't eaten today. I got eggs…"

I don't respond right away. We usually have lunch at 1.00 p.m. but we couldn't because Dad was out.

"I ate," I finally say.

"When?" he asks.

"Ages ago. I had leftovers…"

"And you couldn't wait?" Dad asks, visibly annoyed.

I look at him and I don't know what to say. So I just say, "I'm sorry."

5.11 p.m.

I hear Mum walk through the door just as I'm on the last few pages of my second book. My heart starts beating fast as I race to finish before she comes up to speak to me. I glance at the clock as I read, willing my brain to process the story faster.

When I'm finally done I let out a sigh and fall back on to my pillow.

"Amani!" Mum calls soon after.

I run down to greet her. When I get there her diabetic equipment is out on the table. I frown.

"Don't pull that face at me." Mum chuckles as she pricks her finger to test her insulin levels. I turn away when she sticks the needle in. "I didn't have a chance to stop and eat much today."

"Mum you have to—"

"Oh shush, and give me a hug," she says, pulling me close.

I hug her back a little too intensely and, when we break away, I see her frown over at Dad. He's too busy packing away his laptop to notice.

"Let's go out for food tonight," Dad says. His smile is a little strained.

Mum looks at the clock. "The Italian down the road?" she suggests. "We have enough time for that." She glances at me and I know what she means. So does Dad but none of us address it. "Is that OK, Amani?" Mum asks, and now they're both looking at me, concerned.

"Yeah, of course!" I say. "I just need to get changed." I don't. I just have this thing about leaving the house at fifteen minute intervals. For example 5.00 p.m. or 5.15 p.m. The next slot is 5.30 p.m.

I haven't even told Mum and Dad about this quirk. It's fairly new.

I tried, once, to explain every little thing that preyed on my mind, but Dad scoffed and Mum couldn't understand why some things bothered me and others didn't. I couldn't explain that it's not *me* that decides, it's the OCD. So now I hide anything I can from them.

It's easier.

Only Hermione knows, probably because she's the same. I watch her sometimes and it's like she has an internal alarm clock. She can time things to the minute.

She runs over to me as I enter my room, rubbing her fur against my legs. I found out recently that means she's marking me as her territory.

I bend down and pick her up, burying my face in her fur. She smells like talcum powder and almost immediately I can feel the butterflies in my stomach evaporate.

I sit on my bed, cuddling Hermione, and wait until the time is right.

6.23 p.m.

"Isn't it ready yet?" Mum snaps at the waiter. "It's almost half six."

He's flustered and mumbles something about checking with the chef before retreating to the kitchen.

When he returns he says it'll be another ten minutes and Mum looks like she's about to explode.

"My wife is diabetic, you see," Dad explains, all the while avoiding my gaze.

The truth is my routine means I have to eat at 6.30 p.m. If my food arrives sooner I usually wait. If it arrives later it feels like a balloon is expanding in my stomach, ready to pop. But you can't exactly say, "My daughter has OCD and her mealtimes are planned like clockwork."

The mention of Mum's diabetes does the trick and we're sent some complimentary starters soon after. Just bread and olives, but it's enough to start the ritual.

As the waiter is pouring us some more water, my alarm goes off, signalling dinner time. He startles, spilling water all over the table.

"Amani, for fu—"

"Mark!" Mum's glaring at Dad, who's glaring at me. The waiter backs away, full of apologies. "If you'd just allowed us to eat at home…"

"Don't start with me, Leila," Dad hurls back. "I was

trying to do something nice. The meeting yesterday was awful. I lost the pitch to that start-up."

"Why?" Mum asks, her anger turning to concern. I breathe a sigh of relief. I hate it when they fight over me. "You always win them."

"I was off," Dad admits, and I swear he looks at me. Guilt bubbles up inside of me and I can almost feel the tears, too, but I manage to stop them. "And then my sister came round today and wouldn't stop talking."

Mum curses. "Doesn't she have anything better to do with her time?"

"Apparently not." Dad laughs, and Mum's laughing now, too.

They spend the whole meal chatting about my aunt and her eccentricities, tactfully avoiding asking me about my day, for which I'm thankful.

7.23 p.m.

We're back home. Dad and Mum retreat to the sofa.

"Want to watch a film?" they ask in unison.

"Maybe tomorrow," I say, already halfway up the stairs.

Though we all know that's not going to happen. It's just one of the things we do, where we play at being a normal family.

7.32 p.m.

I lie in bed with my lamp on, staring at the ceiling. All the while my heart is thump, thump, thumping.

7.54 p.m.

I've not moved. My parents are laughing at the film downstairs. I feel detached, like I'm not in control of my body. It's as if they're in a parallel universe to me.

8.28 p.m.

Eventually Hermione whines at me to let her out and I get out of bed, open the door for her, and grab my laptop. I put *Harry Potter and the Philosopher's Stone* on and it feels like my fears slowly ebb away.

9.59 p.m.

I pause the film and start getting ready for bed.

11.32 p.m.

I fall asleep just as Gryffindor wins the house cup and I feel like tomorrow might be a better day.

SUNDAY
7.38 a.m.

When I wake up, I realize I've overslept and, unlike a functional human being, I practically have a breakdown.

I rush to the bathroom to get everything done before 8.00 a.m. I don't even stop to stroke Hermione today and it's only as I'm about to leave my room that I notice she isn't there.

My hand hovers over the chair like I'm about to stroke an invisible cat. I can see little tufts of her fur still there from the day before.

"Mum!" I call. When she doesn't respond I call louder. "MUM!"

I hear hurried footsteps dashing up the stairs. "Amani?" she answers frantically. "What's happened, what's—?" She pauses when she sees me, letting out a breath. "Oh, thank goodness," she says, between pants, holding her hand to her chest. "I thought you… What's wrong?" she asks, rushing over to me.

I'm crying now. Crying again.

"Hermione," I whimper. My chin actually quivers, like in a cartoon. "I can't…" I stop, not voicing what I can't do.

"Stay right there!" Mum says, pulling away. "I'll find her and put her on the chair, and everything will be fine." She's put on her cautious voice, the one she uses when she's worried I'm going to go over the edge.

I wait for some time, my stomach swirling like a whirlpool as the clock ticks on. It's nearly 8.15 a.m. and today's ruined already.

"It's OK, you're OK," I say, squeezing my eyes shut and repeating the words over and over like a chant. I haven't moved from my position by the chair. Eventually I hear Mum's soft footsteps by the door and watch as she carries Hermione through.

She's still sleeping as Mum places her on the chair.

Her breaths come out in pants and she's wheezing a little, like she's having a nightmare.

I want to wake her up and make it stop.

MONDAY
6.53 a.m.

I wake up to a weird scratching noise coming from the corner of my room. It takes me a few moments, in my sleepy state, to notice that it's coming from inside my wardrobe. It's only when I hear her shallow breaths and the same wheezing as yesterday that I realize it must be Hermione. I run over to her right away, forgetting that the floor is lava, and yank open the wardrobe door. She's nuzzling into a pile of discarded clothes, pawing at the wood beneath with her claws. I try to pick her up but she falls limp in my hands. She feels as fragile as a newborn kitten even though she's almost my age.

Something's wrong.

Something's very wrong.

"Mum!" I yell. "Mum!"

I stand there for a few moments, skipping on the spot. But the nuzzling gets worse and Hermione's started making this strange purring noise. I pull open my bedroom door, look at the line that marks the threshold between my room and the hallway, and hover my foot over it.

I step back. I can't.

Then an idea enters my mind. I grab my mobile and call the house phone.

It rings a couple of times and then I hear a gruff voice. "Mu— Dad?" I answer, disappointed.

"Your mum's already left for work, Amani," he says, his voice hoarse. "She isn't your slave. Whatever it is, it can wait."

And he puts the phone down, just like that.

I burst out crying.

I look at the clock. 7.01 a.m. I can't leave for another hour.

I return to Hermione and stroke her as gently as I can, chatting quietly to her. I think it's more of a comfort to me than her.

But it works, a little. She stops nuzzling and all I can hear now is her shallow breathing.

Eventually Dad comes in and finds me curled up next to my wardrobe. I don't see him because my eyelashes are glued together with tears, but I smell his aftershave as he pulls me up from the floor and takes me to Hermione's chair.

"I'm sorry, Amani," he says, and I can hear the guilt in his voice. "I try and understand but I—"

"It's Hermione!" I wail, and Dad turns to where I'm pointing.

He says nothing, just rushes over and inspects her as she starts nuzzling into the corner again. After a few moments he heads for the door. "I'm getting the vet's number," he says, before hurrying down the stairs to the kitchen.

He comes back upstairs less than a minute later and marches over to the wardrobe. "Yes, hello?" Dad says, his voice shaky. "I'm sorry to call so early but…" Dad explains everything – the nuzzling, her breathing, even the fact that she broke her routine yesterday and disappeared. While he talks, I go back and stroke her. I notice that her wheezing sounds more raggedy now, like every breath is painful. "One moment," he says, and he turns to me. "Have you tried to lift her?"

I nod. "She went limp," I explain.

Dad nods back at me and repeats my words to the vet. He pauses while the vet explains something to him. All he says in response is, "Oh no," before leaving my room, and suddenly it feels like a lead brick has landed on my chest. I follow him to the door and lean out. He's all the way down the stairs now. "OK," he finally says. "Yes, I understand. I'll be there in twenty minutes."

Dad walks back up, his steps heavy. He takes me to Hermione's chair again and sits me down. "Amani, I have some bad news," he says, wiping his eyes, and I wait for the words that will confirm my suspicions. "The vet says the symptoms suggest that she's had a … a…" Dad mumbles the word and it takes a moment for the information to sink in.

I run over to Hermione. She's stopped struggling now. I wrap her in an old jumper, gather her in my arms and sit back down on the teal chair, cradling her like a baby.

"I've got to take her now, love," Dad says, crouching

in front of me.

"I'm coming with you," I say.

Dad looks up, slightly surprised. "But you can't…" He turns to the door.

I shake my head. "I'm going."

After a moment, Dad nods. "All right," he says, the strength back in his voice. "I'll just get dressed quickly. See you downstairs?" he asks, uncertain. "Would you like to bring Hermione down?"

I nod through my tears.

Dad leaves. I want to get changed but I also don't want to put her down. I nuzzle into her fur for the last time.

I walk to the door and glance back.

7.23 a.m.

My alarm goes off, signalling that it's time to wake up.

I step out of my bedroom.

ASTOUNDING TALENT! UNEQUALLED PERFORMANCES!

·

Catherine Johnson

Lincolnshire, 1831

The fields behind the house were darkening. There were a few fires where the wagons had been pulled up and tarpaulins stretched out for shelter. In the fading light the fairy ponies, hobbled so they wouldn't stray, seemed to glow.

Devani and Tom saluted as I passed. "Go well, young Darby," Dev called. "Tell Mr B he is in our hearts!" Young Henderson turned away, but Eppie nodded me on, holding up her sister Mariana, for she'd been crying on and off since we'd left Nottingham.

My heart swelled. Born in the workhouse, I had no blood family. But Mr Bassett had given me a family to be proud of. And now he was gone. The least I could do was say farewell.

I came into the house by the back door, since the front had been expressly forbidden to me. Old Mrs Bassett would not be glad to have me in her house at all – and would not know of my presence if I could help it. That woman carried her hatred of me like a girl carries a songbird in a cage, proudly and openly. I moved quietly, slowly, even though I could hear from the voices in the drawing room that Mrs Bassett was engaged in fierce discussion.

The back parlour was empty save for the coffin on the table, and I took off my cap quickly. The man laid out inside was a strange shade between white and yellow. His eyes, under the copper pennies, were sunken in and his jaw had been bound up to prevent it falling open. The room was hung with rosemary and the mirror above the mantelpiece was turned to face the wall. There was no fire in the grate and I was glad of it, for Mr B had been gone these five days past and the weather, for May, was warm.

In the guttering light cast by the tallow candles, he looked little like the man he'd been in life. A good man reduced to a shell.

"Mister Bassett?" I spoke in a whisper, in case one of

the servants was listening at the door.

"I made sure Wonder and Circe were brushed and exercised." I shifted in my seat. There was a stray stalk of hay on my good jacket; I brushed it off. "Oh, they miss you, sir, and no mistake." I sat back in the chair. "We all of us do."

There was no point speaking aloud. Mr Bassett, finest equestrian in the east of England and owner of Bassett's Fair, was truly dead. The doctor who'd confirmed it, a man with a silk top hat and smug bastard face, said it was a brain fever, and that it caused his heart to give up and stop beating.

I myself had been there when Mr Bassett slid sideways off his second-best spotted horse, Circe (though in my way of thinking she was definitely the best), in a sawdust ring behind the market ground in the city of Nottingham. He handed me his hat, the tall felt one with the fine brim, and then his eyes turned up inside his head and there was a sound in the back of his throat I had never heard a man make in my whole eighteen years. Not even when Andreas and Hel, the rope-walkers before me and Susannah, fell from height, walking between the Exchange and the

Shoulder of Mutton Inn in Market Drayton. Even then there'd been nothing like it.

I shook my head. "We promised you a proper send-off, a showman's funeral, but your mother won't have it," I told him.

Normally we'd all watch over the body, the whole company in turn keeping vigil till it was time for burial, but even my coming into the house risked courting Mrs Bassett's ire. It would be impossible for her to miss the entire company sneaking in. I imagined Mariana or one of the other children bursting into tears and the sound bringing Mrs B thundering into the back parlour to find the lot of us crammed in here, circus folk perched on her chairs and tables, holding candles...

The thought made me smile. Mrs Bassett would be furious. And so the vigil was just me. The company had decided it unanimously. It was an honour, for all that I wished it didn't have to be this way.

I finished setting up the candles for the vigil and sat carefully in one of the wooden chairs. I could still hear Mrs Bassett's voice from the front of the house, raised in impatience – I felt bad for whichever servant she was berating.

"I do think," I said, "as she wishes the whole of us would just push off." In fact this was more than a thought, it was an observation, but I thought it better not to inform Mr B so bluntly, given as there was nothing he could do about it. His mother particularly took against the small folk, Tom Thumb and Lucy Clark, her sister and the rest, calling them aberrations. And me. Naturally I was the devil in human form, my skin being an outward badge of the darkness within, and poor Devani, who was both dark-skinned and diminutive, suffered double. Susannah, being almost fair in the ordinary way, and the Hendersons, she tolerated.

Old Mrs Bassett was not a woman who had supped the milk of human kindness. "I wonder, Mr B," I mused. "Perhaps you had her share?"

Mr Bassett said nothing. Around the room the candles guttered and spat. For a second I imagined the shadow cast caused some movement, a contraction in his cheek, and my heart sped up to a gallop.

I cursed under my breath. It was only the flickering light. I sighed and pinched myself for believing in ghosts. Mr Bassett wasn't going anywhere except into the ground in the morning. After he died, every one of us – except for the third and truest to his name of the Three Sensibles, who had family in Nottingham and swore blind his life in the ring was over – had carried him home. Well, to what passed for home. A cold place and a cold-hearted, bitter old woman of a mother.

I leaned on the edge of the coffin and smiled in spite of myself. "You had me there, Mr B," I whispered.

Then the door to the parlour creaked open and I started – to my surprise, I saw it was Susannah, the other rope-walker; she'd stopped, frozen, on the threshold. I pulled her inside, closing the door behind her and put one finger to my lips, willing her quiet.

"What are you doing here?" I hissed. "Did you come in the front way? Did Mrs Bassett see you?"

"The vultures are here," she said, "from Astley's Circus. One of those dark-suited lawyer types, thin as a reed, and his muscled thug. They're in the drawing room, drinking whisky and arguing over the fixtures." She glanced over her shoulder. "I saw them arrive, I thought I might try to change her mind, I thought she liked me—"

"Susannah…"

Her lip trembled. "She's selling everything."

"But the funeral! I thought she'd wait…"

Susannah looked away.

I wanted to hit something. "They have no right!" But even as I said it I knew it was a lie. We were only ever cogs and levers in Mr Bassett's show, to people like her.

I blinked and rubbed my face. I was as helpless as the dead man. I pulled out a chair for Susannah and she sat. I reached out and put my hand on her shoulder.

"Maybe Astley's will have places for some of us in London?" I tried to paint a brighter picture.

She flapped a hand and shrugged me off. "They have enough tightrope walkers and dancers, thank you. And enough Lilliputians, too. Astley's man took great pleasure informing me they have riders aplenty for the fairy ponies, which they do want."

I went to speak but she cut me off.

"They want all the horses, from the tinies to the Spotted Wonders. Oh, and they've asked for Aris and Rima Elliot. The trapeze is the thing in London, apparently. But clowns and rope-walkers are two a penny." Her tone was sharp.

I thought of Circe. "All the horses?"

She looked hard at me. "William Darby... Do you think to steal her and run?"

My shoulders sagged. "No – no, of course not. But perhaps..." I sighed. "Surely this doesn't have to mean the end of the circus. We have bookings every month for the summer – Newark, Mansfield, up to Yorkshire. I was hoping..." She almost laughed at me then but I protested, "We have a good show!"

"Oh, and you imagine we can all of us walk across country and roll up with no horses? An equestrian extravaganza without equines?"

"We've rope-walkers, the Hendersons, you. And clowns, Asmo, and two of the Sensibles..." But I knew there would be no show without the horses. Even if by some miracle I could get Circe away ... one would not be enough. Susannah knew it, too. She met my eyes with knowing sadness and the two of us sat in silence for a moment, in the flickering light of the cheap candles. I realized now that the other voice I could hear must be Astley's lawyer.

Next to me, Susannah sighed and let her face sink

into her hands. "I thought she'd listen," she said again. "I don't understand, she'll listen to Astley's people – have them in her good parlour, even! Aren't they circus folk, too?"

I scoffed bitterly. "Astley's? I am sure she thinks them a better class of showpeople, who have performed for Princess Adelaide and do not travel the country like vagabonds." I shook my head and sighed.

"You should go back to the others," I said. "They need you more than I do. Comfort Mariana for me; I cannot leave yet."

"Will..."

"Please," I said.

Susannah bit her lip and got to her feet. The door closed softly behind her. It was just me and Mr B again.

"What d'you reckon, Mr B? How do we get out of this one? I have no wish to return to the workhouse." I sat down again. "You remember picking me out?" I said. "I remember you, tallest stovepipe hat I had ever seen, all big words and wearing that showman's coat with velvet trim. You wanted a boy with decent balance and bearing." I swallowed. There seemed to be a lump in my throat. "These folk are family now,"

I told him. "The only one I have. I have no intention of losing them."

I got up off the chair and walked the crack in the wooden floor as if I was on the high wire. One foot in front of the other, imagining I was stepping out into nothing, hands stretched out either side. Making my mind clear. There had to be a way through this. A way that would see old Mrs Bassett with the money she craved and us showpeople with a living. I took a deep breath and centred myself, as I would if I were twenty yards up.

Then the door swung open suddenly and I wobbled sideways, knocking into the table and skewing the coffin almost clean off it.

I struggled to pull it back. "Susannah!" But it was not Susannah. "Mrs Bassett! Please, forgive me."

Her eyes shot daggers. She was a small, round woman, dressed in black, with white lace lappets like rabbits ears falling either side of her face. Any other day I would have laughed at the set of her mouth and her pinprick eyes. She was carrying a light, and she was not alone – a slender man with a pinched look followed in her wake.

I imagined the scene from outside. A young man with arms out either side of him as if making play, and I knew that if there had been any chance of talking her round, of asking for delay in the sale, of any kind of help, it had flown as soon as she saw me in that room.

Her voice was low as a serpent and just as cold. "Get out of my house."

I bowed low. "Madam, sir." I did not move. "The tradition, Mrs Bassett. A vigil—" I began.

"Your traditions are of no importance! And you are not welcome."

"But Madam—"

"And another thing. I want none of you at the funeral. Do you know the shame he brought me? My son the showman? He was a disgrace."

It felt like I was falling. Falling off the high wire and seeing the ground rush up to meet me. I tried pleading. "Madam, I beg you, spare the show. We will pay, of course. The fairy horses will pine without Lucy and Tom Thumb…"

"He trashed our good name. I thank God my son is dead. He can do no more harm." She spat the words.

I saw my own shock reflected in the face of Astley's

man – for I presumed that's who her companion was.

"I would not take a penny of your tainted money." She turned on her heel. "Kotting, fetch your man to throw this devil out."

After a moment's hesitation, Kotting called out and a man so wide he filled the doorframe came down the corridor. He was bigger than our strongman, with hair in a halo round his face. A man crossed with a lion.

Mrs Bassett's face was a picture of self-righteousness. "Take him out."

The giant lifted me up by my collar and my good shirt tore.

"No!" My legs were windmilling in the air. Mr Kotting nodded at his man, who said nothing.

"Please!" He walked me out of the door and down the steps into the yard in front of the house. He put me down but kept one massive hand curled around my arm. I tried to shake him off but my effort was useless. He could have snapped my arm in two if he'd wanted, without breaking a sweat.

Beyond the outbuildings, the barn and the carriage house, I could hear the lament for Mr B coming from our camp. It was 'The Motherless Child', which always made me cry. I felt my face grow hot and my lungs empty.

"You can let me go," I said to the lion man. I was surprised when he smiled kindly.

"I don't agree with the old woman," he said, his English accented, "but the boss has come for the horses."

"We are good people," I said.

He loosened his grip. "I was born in a circus. Astley's are good people, too."

I shook my head. "They're destroying Mr Bassett's work, the show..."

"You have your limbs, you can still work. You're Young Darby, aren't you? I have seen your name on the bills. Negro Rope Dancer and Horseman."

I could not help the tiny bubble of pride that came from being recognized. Then I immediately felt foolish for allowing myself such a worthless emotion.

"They are my family."

He said nothing for a long while. Then he nodded. "Life is cruel, young man. Now, if I let you go, will you have a drink with me? Leave the old woman and my master to make their deal?"

"Our tradition is to keep a vigil with the dead. I hate to think of Mr B alone tonight."

The lion man shrugged. "He is dead. It is the living who need looking after now." He let me go and took a flask from inside his jacket. We settled on the bank at the side of the road and he took a sip and passed the flask to me. It smelled, I do not lie, like hell. But I tipped back my head and, as the liquor went burning down my throat, it warmed me.

"Astley's business is nonpareil." The lion man took another drink. "Their stables are bigger than the household cavalry and clean enough to eat off the floor." He sighed. "But I miss the travel. A new town every week, the camaraderie of the road."

I looked at him. "Are you French?"

He shrugged again. "Spanish, French. I am a London man now, I think." He leaned back to look at the stars.

"Our horses belong with us," I said. Up in the night sky I thought I saw a shooting star. Was that a good omen or ill? I shut my eyes. I had sat under the stars like this so often in the past, travelling the length and breadth of England with Bassett's Circus, and the night sky was the same now as it had been every one of those nights. Could everything really be so final? Perhaps it was leaving Mrs Bassett's miserable house that made me think this way, or perhaps it was the spirits already beginning to take effect – but the lion man's voice cut across my thoughts either way.

"Mr Darby." He handed me the flask. "If I were in your shoes, I would fight."

I sat up and drank. "Fight you?" I asked.

He laughed. "Fight the world. Ach, you will have to do it one way or another. You are a black man in a white world. A foreigner."

The remark stung. "I was born in Norwich," I told him.

He raised an eyebrow and I sat up, indignant. "This country is as much mine as any other Englishman's. This – this soil," I said, taking a handful of earth from the bank in my fingers, "you see this soil? This land? From north to south, all mine." I took in a deep breath, looking again at the stars, and let my head fall back against the bank, squeezing the cool damp earth between my fingers. "And what is more, those spotted horses? They are mine, too! This show, these people you would scatter and uproot, they are family!"

The man shook his head. "I doubt if anyone else sees it that way." And then he smiled and winked at me. "So you have nothing to lose, I think."

For a moment I imagined rounding up the company and rushing the house, showing Mr Kotting and old Mrs Bassett and anyone else that together we were unstoppable, incredible – that we were, as the bills said, electrifying.

I marched towards the house where the lanterns blazed at the front door. I was halfway across the yard when Kotting came out; he was shaking Mrs Bassett's hand, a sheaf of papers almost spilling from his briefcase. I heard him tell her he would send a transport for the livestock at the end of the week.

The front door shut hard. Kotting turned, a smile on his face. He looked past me to where his lion man was getting up and putting on his hat.

"Bring the trap round, would you, Pablo?" Kotting said, as if I was not there.

With every fibre of my being I had to force myself not to knock him down. I almost shouted but stopped myself just in time. What would I say? What possible way could I get what I wanted?

The trap, with Pablo driving and its lamps lit, rounded the side of the house. Kotting eyed me nervously. I thought of the funeral tomorrow. It was so tempting to imagine coming to the church in spite of Mrs Bassett's wishes, to swing my fists at any man who tried to keep me and the others from attending our Mr Bassett's funeral – but for all Pablo had said that I should fight, I knew I could not gain any advantage with my knuckles or with force. What else did I have? Fine words? My mouth was dry and no words came. I watched the trap pull away out of the yard and down to the road.

They had gone.

•

I woke with a headache. The sunlight was fierce; it seemed to shine directly into my head through my eyeballs and scour my skull. But Susannah had no pity – she forced me up and into my decent jacket. I put on Mr Bassett's hat and pulled it down over my eyes.

Then we made a procession: the Elliots, the Hendersons, Asmodens walking with the remaining two Sensibles, and then the small folk, all of us in our blacks. Eppie carried Mariana on her hip, and Lucy and Tom Thumb and Devani walked with me and Susannah. Dev wore a black veil that almost reached the grass – she looked unearthly, a spirit girl. Tom said she was already weeping, not only for Mr Bassett, but for the loss of her favourite pony. I told her I felt the same about Circe.

"Mr B would be spinning in his grave if he knew we were going to be parted," Devani said between sobs, and Susannah rubbed her hand and told her – barefaced lies I thought – that all would be well in the end.

We made our way across the fields, a ragged procession of different shades of black, like poor crows, to the church gate where a red-faced farmer's boy told us we were not welcome inside as Mrs Bassett had requested a private funeral. I felt the guilt pierce me like a stone arrow. I took the young man aside. He was about the same age as me. "It is my fault," I told him. "But let the others in that they might pay their respects. He was like a father to us." But the boy would not move an inch.

Aris and the younger Henderson would have fought

him and stormed the service. Tom Thumb was burning with anger. He looked up at the farmer's boy. "We are his flesh and blood!" he said.

The farmer's boy smirked and, if Susannah had not held me back, I swear I would have knocked him down.

"We will bide our time," she whispered. "That woman will have you locked up if you give her cause."

She was right, of course. We withdrew beyond the wall of the graveyard. Some of the children fell asleep in the sun and Devani put up her veil. Asmo took out his violin and played the saddest song he knew. We, all of us, wept.

It was half an hour before the handful of mourners emerged into the sun, and we waited again while the sexton and the gravedigger lowered the coffin into the ground. Mrs Bassett threw a handful of dirt after her son and left, not looking back.

I was first to the grave, my hat in my hands. I had been minded by Susannah to say a few words, but it was hard. There was too much sadness choking my throat and squeezing my chest tight. She gave me a stare and I nodded, steeling myself.

I looked around the company once more, took a breath. "Brothers, sisters," I began, and my voice cracked. Susannah reached for my hand.

"Mr Bassett was a fine showman," I said. "The finest. I'm sure you'll agree it was an honour and a privilege to work for him. We were his people. His family." I looked up and a mob of swifts wheeled and chased, calling to each other and scything the sky. They were so fast, so quick, so joyful. Tiny but unstoppable, riding the gusts and winds sending them this way and that but never ceasing. I looked at Tom, his lip wobbling, and the Sensibles, grim-faced. Susannah was blinking away tears. Devani began to wail. I thought I would, too. I could feel the hurt pushing up.

In the sky the swifts called again. They almost sounded mocking. Maybe they thought we were idiots. What had the lion man, Pablo, said? That I would always have to fight? Well, that was the truth. But didn't these people deserve my fighting, too? I put on Mr Bassett's hat. "Mr B would not have wanted this. He would have wanted us to stay together. The horses, the Elliots..."

Asmo gave me a look. "Old news." He sighed, his

face sad and beaten as only a clown's face can be. "I'll tour no more... Perhaps I'll carve spoons instead."

Devani took his hands. "Asmo, dear. You are the best clown in the north. Just because London does not want us..."

A swift screamed overhead. I blinked. "We all would stay together..." I began.

"Aye, if there was a chance to work," Aris said and Rima, by his side, nodded.

Young Henderson shaded the sun from his eyes. "We need the horses, Will."

Tom Thumb looked grim. "This time next month they'll be in London. No more green fields."

"London!" I said. "Of course!" It was as if the swift had dropped the idea into my head. "Astley's does not tour!"

"So?" Susannah made a face.

"We make a deal. We offer to pay Astley's a cut of our takings. We have the dates. We buy the horses back, bit by bit. We stay together."

Devani's eyes were round. "Would it work?"

"If we don't ask, we'll never know!" I started for the road that led back to Bassett's farm. "I'm going to talk to Kotting." I called. "One last chance."

"The London stage leaves at two," Susannah said. "They'll have left town by the time…"

"I'm taking Circe," I said.

Susannah picked up her skirts and ran to catch up. "I'm coming, too."

"You'll be too late!" I think it was Aris who called out but I didn't look round. "They could be halfway to London by now!"

I ignored them – I wasn't ready to give up. I ran to the yard behind the house and saddled Circe double-quick. Susannah hauled herself up, in full mourning, on to Wonder. By the time we rode out, the rest of our party had made their way back from the graveyard and I could see the Hendersons hitching their wagon and Tom Thumb in the lower field, arms out, whistling to the fairy ponies.

Susannah looked at me. "Come on!"

I kicked my heels and Circe pricked her ears. We headed cross-country at full gallop towards town. We fairly flew across the fields, horses flattened out and so fast it seemed they knew all our futures were at stake. As we passed the swifts swooped and called as if they were flying with us.

We clattered to a halt outside the inn in the high street. A boy was clearing away the mess of six horses and I knew we'd missed them. I saw my despair reflected in Susannah's face and tried not to let it show in my own. I turned Circe.

"The London road," I said. "We can catch them up." And Susannah was off almost ahead of me. But the road was dry and hard, and we were forced to slow our pace to an uneven trot between the furrows left by a thousand wagons and carts. A single magpie's rattling cry cut the air. I looked for its partner but there was none. A promise of bad luck. Perhaps we would not catch them after all.

But as we turned the corner before the Newark crossroads, I almost fell off Circe there and then. Susannah pulled up Wonder and looked at me, mouth open.

Blocking the road in all directions around the London stage were the Hendersons' wagon, the Elliots' wagon; Asmodens walking on his two high stilts, long tattered coat flying; and a string of gleaming fairy ponies and their riders with Devani and Tom Thumb at their head. They had shed their mourning dress as quickly as they would have changed costumes in the ring, and their red and gold dragoons' uniforms shone in the sunlight. My heart leaped. No one could say that Bassett's company did not know how to put on a spectacle.

The driver was swearing the air bright blue with all the oaths known to man, and waving the coachmen to clear the road. But my family did not move one inch. I slid off Circe and made my way through.

Beside me and all around me I felt something like a kind of electricity flowing out of my family, my friends, my brothers and sisters of the road. It made me feel as if I could do anything at all.

"Mr Kotting! Mr Kotting, sir!" I called out. The leather blind at the stagecoach window flew up. There was Pablo the lion man, his shaggy head filling the space, grinning. The driver swore again.

I drew closer as Pablo opened the door and jumped down. "Young Darby. I thought you'd never come."

"Pablo." I bowed low, sweeping Mr Bassett's hat off my head.

Mr Kotting stepped down behind him. He looked

around at all of us, his face sour.

"These horses," he said. "They are Astley's now. Any damages or injury will have to be paid for…"

"Mr Kotting, I beg you. We all beg you." I looked from the lion man to Kotting and held his gaze as steady as I could. "A deal. We lease the horses. Give us four months. We already have shows lined up across the north. If we haven't paid in full by the autumn, the animals are yours."

Mr Kotting sighed. The horses, waiting, pawed the ground and snorted. There was the clank of bits and rattle of traces. I thought I heard the magpie again. The driver spat and cursed once more but I did not look away.

I offered him my hand. Time seemed to stop. Every single one of us held our breath.

"Sir?" I said.

William Darby was born in 1811, in the workhouse in Norwich. His father was listed as a butler, probably imported as a slave. His parents died when William Darby was a baby. Aged eleven he was apprenticed to

William Batty, a circus owner, and performed as Young Darby, Negro Rope Dancer and Equestrian. He became one of the country's top showmen, running his own circus, and bred some of the best dancing (dressage) horses in the UK. When he began his own circus he performed under the name Pablo Fanque's Circus and, after appearing in front of Queen Victoria added the title 'Royal'. In the mid-nineteeth century he was a massive celebrity and probably the finest horseman of his age.

Black and Minority Ethnic Britons have been a part of this country since Roman times (and before). Pablo Fanque is just one of the most visible.

I always wondered how he chose his stage name…

HACKNEY MOON
·
Tanya Byrne

You're under no obligation to be the same person you were five minutes ago

– Alan Watts

I want to tell you a story about a girl called Esther. It doesn't matter why I chose her, why I choose any of you, because there's no magic in that, is there? No, the magic is in knowing that something outside of you, something beyond the reach of your oh-so-fragile fingers, is conspiring with the universe to make sure that you're OK. You need to know that you're not alone, don't you? That *this* isn't it, that somewhere out there, someone sees you.

I see you.

I see you like I saw Esther that day.

Do you want to know what I saw?

Of course you do.

•

Later, Esther will look back and realize how appropriate it was that it happened on New Year's Eve. The truth is: it wasn't an accident. Nothing I do is an accident. I'm telling you that now, before we go any further, so you know not to question my intentions. You will, of course – everyone does – and that's OK. It's OK not to trust me. Just because I want something to happen, doesn't mean you can't put up a fight.

There will be times when you will ask yourself, why her? Why Esther? It's true, there are other stories I could tell you. Bigger, brighter stories of love and lust and stardust, but when you ask yourself, *Why her?* consider this: why *not* her? History doesn't remember people like Esther, just like it doesn't remember people like you, people who live and love and laugh without disturbing the equilibrium of the universe. And that's OK because there are parts of your story that you don't want told. Scars in places not everyone can see.

I see. You don't want me to but I can. And, in a hundred years, when history is telling someone else's story, I'll remember yours. Your life might be ordinary, but you are anything but. You think there's nothing remotely special about you. Little old ordinary you with your cracked phone screen and your thirsty heart. But you are made up of a thousand tiny marvellous pieces. All those defeats and wins and wounds. Every lie you've told, every time you tried *so hard* and wanted it *so much* but it wasn't enough. Every time you loved someone but they didn't love you back. Like Esther, you are broken and beautiful and I see you, too.

I see.

•

Before we can go forwards, we must go back, just a few months, to September and the first day of the school year. Esther was late because she had waited for Sam to knock for her. Who's Sam? Well, Sam was Sam and she broke Esther's heart – that's all you need to know for now. Sam didn't knock for her and if Esther was honest with herself, she knew that was going to happen. After all, she hadn't seen Sam since the last day of term, on that bright afternoon in July when the summer rolled out at their feet like a red carpet.

Sam did that a lot – came and went – but she always came back eventually, like a restless cat that turned up when it was hungry. This time she didn't but Esther still hoped, so when she went into the toilets at school to check if Sam was there, I felt obliged to give her a nudge. I'm not saying I have the power to control who uses what cubicle but say I engineered it so that the one by the window, the one where Esther and Sam had written their initials in black Sharpie, was free. And say Esther went in and saw that someone had added ARE LEZZAS underneath. That would be bad enough, wouldn't it? The whole school knowing she was gay when she hadn't even said it out loud yet. But what if someone had crossed it out? Esther would know then, right? She'd know that Sam had seen it first, that she was freaking out, which is why she'd run away to Cyprus for the summer and not told her. She'd know once and for all that it – whatever 'it' was or could have been – was over.

You no doubt think I'm cruel. But what about letting someone think that's how love is supposed to be? That's cruel. You see, all the books and films and songs had told Esther that love was confusing and complicated and inconvenient; that if it didn't hurt, she wouldn't be able to feel it. She didn't know that you could love someone without having to change. Poor, sweet Esther who was half Guyanese and half English and told herself that she was not enough of either to be one hundred per cent anything. She was so used to feeling like she didn't fit anywhere that she didn't know you could love someone without watching everything you say and do.

Without making yourself smaller and quieter until you become invisible.

Esther thought she had to fit *around* Sam, to fill her in; that her love would be the cement that could fix each of Sam's cracks and make her stronger. But love isn't cement, is it? It can't fix people. Love can give you a *reason* to want to fix someone – even to fix yourself – but it isn't enough on its own. You can love someone with every bit of your heart but you can't change them. The only one that kind of love changes is you. I've seen it so many times. It hurts until it doesn't, I don't know what else to tell you. Esther thought it hurt so much because she and Sam were supposed to be together, but what no one had told her was that the pain would pass.

Everything heals, I swear. Everything. Bones mend and bruises fade and hearts repair themselves. But Esther was sixteen and the taste of heartbreak was still fresh in her mouth. She thought she'd feel that way forever. That's why I stepped in. If Esther hadn't seen what was written in that cubicle, this story would have ended very differently.

•

They didn't speak that first week of school. Esther tried. Sam didn't. If you want to know how a relationship ends, sometimes it's as simple as that: one tries and the other doesn't. That's it. I don't know how else to put it.

Are you thinking about someone right now? I know you are. Come on, close your eyes and tell me about them, about how they make you feel. If you can't – or, if you're brave enough to be honest, you *won't* – then you have more in common with Esther than you think. She would do the same, sit in the art room at school by herself trying not to think about Sam. She'd let her chips go cold as she tried to distract herself from checking her phone, scrubbing at sheets of sugar paper until they tore, until she gave herself tender blisters on her fingers from the oil pastels. Always dark colours; blue and black and purple and sometimes just red.

Red.

Red.

Red.

If she wasn't there, she was at home. I often found her sitting in the garden, looking up at the moon. She would reach out sometimes and let the moonlight silver her fingers. When she turned her wrist, she was sure she could feel the chill of it against her skin, as though she'd dipped her hand into the lake at Vicky Park. Each time she pulled back she expected to bring a palmful of moonlight with her but her hand would be empty. It was the same way she felt every time she touched Sam, like she couldn't be sure it had happened at all.

•

So that's how it ended – not with a bang but with a squiggle of graffiti. The truth is, Esther wasn't entirely surprised by what had been written in the toilet cubicle. There had always been rumours. Nothing Esther couldn't handle, winking and giggling and bawdy remarks about how much time she and Sam used to spend together. She usually laughed it off but by the time they were due to break up for the summer, the comments about Esther's relationship with Sam had become an everyday occurrence. The boys would quiz them for tips on giving head and the girls would ask them if they wanted to be alone in the shower after hockey practice.

What had felt like playful banter had become something that made Sam blush and take a step away from her. That's when it stopped being something they could laugh off. "It'd help if you didn't dress like such a dyke," Sam would tell her every time one of the boys offered them a tenner to watch and Esther would laugh, but she knew Sam meant it. So that September, when she saw that Sam had scrubbed out what had been written in the toilets, Esther knew she wouldn't hear from her again. But it still hurt when Sam sat somewhere else in maths, when she walked past her in the corridor and when she let Jordan Chapman finger her at his seventeenth in an effort to prove how heterosexual she was. Eventually Esther had to ask herself how much a person has to change before they become someone else. It was almost as if Sam was gone, as if her best friend had died and there was a new girl at school who kind of looked like her – a new girl who laughed too loud and wore lipstick the colour of a fresh cut, which she'd leave behind on everything – tissues and coffee cups and boys' necks.

•

She and Sam always used to hang out at the weekend, so that first Saturday, Esther made sure she had plans. There was a thing at Rich Mix in Shoreditch about DIY Culture that Sam never would have gone to, so Esther went. It was busier than she expected, the narrow pavement cluttered with people smoking and handing out leaflets for demonstrations. They were the sort of people Sam usually took the piss out of. Mostly women with nose rings and hand-poked tattoos, who, Esther realized with sudden, painful clarity, kind of looked like her. In her jeans and *Thrasher* T-shirt, she didn't look out of place among them. It had been a long time since she'd felt like that.

She got her hand stamped by a woman with blue hair and wandered through the double doors into the main space. It was even busier inside – so busy she wasn't sure that she'd be able to move much further. She'd been to Rich Mix loads of times, usually to the cinema, when she could persuade Sam to stay in the same place for two hours, or by herself to exhibitions when she couldn't, but she'd never seen it so packed. She could hear someone talking and got up on tiptoes, peering over heads to find four women onstage, sitting across two black leather sofas. According to the screen behind them, it was a talk on DIY Justice and she scanned the rows of fold-up chairs for an empty space. There wasn't one, so she was forced to join the people who had gathered into a horseshoe at the back. She was too short to see anything, though, and even with the mic, it was difficult to hear what the women were saying over the eager hum. So she stepped back, hoping to find a quiet spot to stand in as she felt an all-too-familiar pop of anxiety suddenly fizz in her chest.

The last time she'd felt like this was at a party Sam had dragged her to in Streatham. She had wanted to dance but the living room was so full they couldn't move. The next morning, Esther had found bruises on her arms and legs from where she had to shove her way out. The memory of it made her mouth go dry and her head spin so suddenly she saw stars, as she realized she might have to do the same thing now. But just as she was sure that her legs were about to give way, she saw something through the crowd – a flash of yellow on the other side of the room. It wasn't just yellow, it was *yellow*. Custard yellow. Rubber-duck yellow. Happy yellow.

Esther moved towards it.

It was a bit of a blur and she had to barge past a few people in an effort to free herself from the crowd. But as she got closer and closer to the blur of yellow she felt better, like the sun appearing on an overcast day to warm the back of your neck. The tightness in her chest eased and when she finally reached a table to find a girl in a bright yellow jumper sitting behind it, the relief was giddying.

"Hey." The girl smiled so wide Esther could see the gap between her teeth. She was black with a froth of curls not unlike her own. She handed Esther something. It was a zine, not unlike the one Esther made herself. It was smaller, though, the hand-drawn title and cover illustration printed on turquoise paper that was folded so it almost fitted in the palm of her hand. Esther looked up to find that the whole space was edged with similar tables, each of them covered in handmade zines and comics. Some people were selling T-shirts as well, and badges and sew-on patches. She even saw a sign that said, 'Poems £1'. She'd heard that people would be selling their stuff there, but she had no idea there would be this many. If she'd got her shit together instead of worrying about Sam, she could have done the same.

"It's about *Chewing Gum*," the girl in the yellow jumper said, tugging Esther's attention away from an illustration of Harry Potter as a black kid on the other side of the room. When Esther looked back, she realized that the girl was wearing black lipstick. Esther always wished she was brave enough to wear black lipstick.

"*Chewing Gum*," the girl repeated, slower this time.

"Like *Extra*?"

"Not chewing gum." Esther must have looked even more confused because the girl arched an eyebrow at her. "*Chewing Gum* the *show* on E4 with Susie Wokoma."

Esther shrugged.

The girl didn't look impressed. "Just take it," she said, waving her hand at her. "Educate yourself."

"I'll swap you," Esther suggested, shrugging her backpack off her shoulder. As she unzipped it and reached in, the sleeve of her jacket moved up to reveal part of the tattoo on her right forearm.

"Let me see." The girl didn't wait, reaching over for Esther's wrist and pulling it towards her. She shoved her sleeve up to her elbow and said, "That's cool. Did you design it?"

"Nah. It's copied from something I drew but Carl Sagan designed it."

"Carl Sagan?"

"He was an astronomer."

"What is it?"

"A Pioneer plaque."

"A Pioneer plaque?"

"It's kind of like a map. It was onboard Pioneer 10 when it launched in 1972."

"Why?"

"In case Pioneer 10 was intercepted. It tells aliens where we are in the universe."

"No, I mean why did you get a tattoo of it?"

"So aliens know where I am."

"Why do you want aliens to know where you are?"

"Why wouldn't I?"

The girl tilted her head from side to side then nodded. "Fair enough."

"I'm a bit obsessed with aliens," Esther confessed when the girl finally let go of her wrist. "I edit a zine as well. I sell it online with my artwork and stuff."

She pulled one out of her backpack. The girl took it and frowned. "1013?"

"It's an *X Files* thing. I want to be Dana Scully when I grow up."

The girl didn't look up.

"Everyone thinks I'm weird," Esther added to fill the silence as the girl flicked through it.

"I like weird," she said, chuckling at an illustration of the Mona Lisa with an alien's face.

"Yeah?"

The girl didn't reply so Esther took it as her cue to leave, heaving her backpack on to her shoulder again.

But just as she was about to walk away, the girl looked up. "You staying for the whole thing?"

Esther shrugged. "I dunno."

"If you are –" she took back her zine, turned it over and wrote down her number – "my mates and I are heading out afterwards. You should come with us. We specialize in weird."

"Oh," Esther said. "OK."

The girl extended her hand. "I'm Alesha, by the way. Alesha Ambrose."

"Esther." She shook it. "Esther Baptiste."

"Nice to meet you, Esther Baptiste."

Sometimes it's as simple as that.

•

I'm not saying I had anything to do with them meeting… But say I did, and say I knew that Esther was going to bottle it. You'd intervene, right? Of course you would. It's not like I did anything dramatic but sometimes these situations call for some courage. So I gave Esther the courage to text Alesha.

Much to her surprise – and delight – Alesha responded immediately, suggesting they meet outside Rich Mix half an hour later. She made her wait forty minutes but just as Esther was about to leg it, Alesha tumbled out with her friends in a rush of light and laughter. It had started to rain so her yellow jumper looked even brighter in the dull light of the Bethnal Green Road – so bright that if Esther could've looked away, she would have.

"Hey, babe," Alesha said, stopping in front of her.

Esther's heart stopped. *Babe.* Had she forgotten her name?

"This is Leomie." She thumbed at the girl on her left, then did the same to the girl standing on her right. "And this is Bee. Guys, this is Esther."

Esther.

Her heart started again, twice as fast.

"You ready, Ess?" Alesha smiled and it felt like she was falling. It was all Esther could do not to reach out for her hand to steady herself.

She nodded. "Yeah."

And she was.

•

They went to a café on Brick Lane, drank Coke straight from the can and talked. There was no awkwardness, no idle chitchat, no "So what school do you go to?"

Esther just pulled up a chair and sat with them.

Her own group of friends (until it whittled down to just Sam) was pretty mixed, but this was the first time Esther had hung out with just black girls. Everything about them was loud. They talked loudly, laughed loudly, even drank loudly, hitting their cans on the table when Bee roasted Alesha for her shoes.

"My grandma has shoes like that," Bee told her.

Alesha sipped her Coke. "Your grandma has taste."

"My grandma has cataracts."

When they laughed, Alesha broke into patois to tell them to shut up. Esther had never hung around with anyone who spoke patois before and it was a joy to hear. Listening to the three of them go back and forth was like being in her grandmother's kitchen, her aunts teasing each other while they made pholourie.

Esther realized that the other people in the café were looking at them – at Bee in her blue lipstick and Alesha in her jumper and Leomie with her shaved head and T-shirt that said BLACK GIRL MAGIC. But she didn't care. They were magic. All of them. And for the first time in her short, bright life, Esther felt like she fitted. All those times in the past when she had checked her phone for a message or, at school, when she looked across the canteen at Sam, I wanted to tell her that she was so young, that there were things she hadn't even felt yet, tell her to be patient because it was coming. Just wait. She wouldn't have listened, though, so I had to show her. So that Saturday afternoon in that tiny café on Brick Lane, she saw. She knew then what a remarkable thing it is to find pieces of yourself in other people. It doesn't happen often but one day – if you're lucky, like Esther – you'll meet someone who'll make it so easy to be yourself, you'll wonder why you ever pretended to be anyone else.

•

She didn't see Alesha again until the following Saturday. Bee wanted to take some shots of Leomie for the next issue of her zine and Esther suggested Dalston Eastern Curve Garden, so they met there and took photos until it got dark. Afterwards they ended up in a bookshop in Haggerston, drank coffee and ate bagels and chatted about books. Esther mostly listened as they talked about Audre Lorde and Sojourner Truth, names she'd never heard. It was the first time since she'd met them that she didn't feel part of the conversation and she found herself shrinking back in her chair.

Alesha must have noticed because she turned to her and said, "I mean, look at Picasso."

Esther swallowed a mouthful of bagel and frowned. "Picasso?"

"You're into art, right, Ess?"

She nodded.

"Picasso straight up stole work from African artists."

"Right? The definition of cultural appropriation." Bee pointed her coffee cup at her. "He was considered a creative visionary while the African artists he was inspired by died anonymous and broke."

Esther didn't know what cultural appropriation was nor had she ever been moved to consider what had inspired Picasso's African Period. It hadn't occurred to her that it might have been other artists.

While Bee and Leomie deliberated over whether to get another coffee, Alesha leaned in and whispered, "There's a talk at the Tate Modern about it next month. Wanna go?"

"Yeah." Esther smiled and when Alesha smiled back,

she was glad she was sitting down because it felt like she was falling again.

•

The four of them were inseparable after that. They watched films at the Curzon and lost Sunday afternoons sitting in coffee shops talking about everything from make-up and music to the varied and cunning ways their anxiety was trying to ruin their lives. It was nice; better than nice, it was comforting. After years of watching everything she said and did – especially when she was with Sam – it was a relief not to overthink everything and just be.

The first time she and Alesha held hands was at the bookshop in Haggerston, the one where they'd talked about Picasso. They were in the basement, listening to a poet, when Alesha reached for her hand. She turned to look at her as she did and when Esther smiled sloppily, as if she'd had too much wine, Alesha didn't let go.

•

If things were going so well, you're probably wondering why I stuck around. I'd done my bit after all. But the first time they kissed, at the bus stop on the Kingsland Road, the rain tapping steadily on the shelter, Esther got home and checked her phone to find a notification. It was just a like on a selfie she'd taken at a Stormzy gig at Halloween but it was enough to knock the breath right out of her for the second time that evening.

Esther had no idea how Sam knew about Alesha. She'd posted photographs of her, of course, but some of her family – here and in Guyana – followed her on Instagram so she was always discreet. But there she was.

sam.ridley liked your post. 2h

Her timing, as always, was impeccable.

It started with that one like; then, when Esther didn't respond, she liked another photo and the next day another and the day after that another and on and on until Esther got the message: Sam was back.

She ignored her but by Christmas Eve, Sam'd had enough and sent the text Esther had been dreading.

I miss you.

Esther ignored that, too.

•

It was the day before New Year's Eve, that strange period after Christmas when no one quite knows what to do with themselves. The decorations were still up but they looked weird somehow. Silly. After all, Christmas was over and there was nothing to look forward to. Soon they'd be back at school, the presents and parties and afternoon naps in front of the telly a mere memory.

Not that Esther and Alesha cared. They were on their way to a birthday party in Stratford and were almost twenty minutes late to meet Bee and Leomie because they kept stopping in the street to laugh and kiss. They told them that the bus broke down and Leomie rolled her eyes. "The absolute state of you two," she said with a chuckle, clocking their messed-up hair and what remained of their lipstick that hadn't been kissed away.

The party was off Carpenters Road. They could hear the music from half a mile away. Inside it was rammed, which made dancing difficult, but they persisted until it got too much and they had to retreat to the kitchen. As soon as they did, Bee and Leomie started chatting to someone they went to school with and Alesha took the chance, grabbing a beer off the kitchen counter, then taking Esther's hand and leading her out into the garden. They found a spot at the side of the house and spent the rest of the night kissing in between sips of Red Stripe.

"Let's stay here forever," Esther whispered into her hair, fingers skimming over Alesha's shoulders. They were as brown and smooth as the head of a sparrow, she thought, pressing her mouth to Alesha's throat. Alesha's skin was so warm it made her sigh. It was always warm and smelled of shea butter and something else, something that made her want to press her nose into the curve of her neck and inhale.

Esther knew everything about her now – how she was scared of clowns and open water, about the mole on the back of her neck that looked like a drop of ink, and how the fine baby hairs that haloed her forehead felt against her fingers. She knew secret things about her as well, things no one else knew; the scar on the back of her knee and the sound she made every time Esther ran her tongue along her collarbone. Alesha knew these things about her as well. She said the birthmark on the inside of her thigh was the shape of

Guyana and that the stretch marks clawing over her hips looked cool, like lightning.

Letting someone touch you where it scares you – is that love? Esther often asked herself.

She thought it might be.

●

When Esther got home that night, drunk on Red Stripe and Alesha, her heels hanging from her fingers, Sam was sitting on the wall outside her house.

"What are you doing here?"

Sam just looked at her. "My dad died."

●

Esther's parents were in bed so she told Sam to be quiet as she reached for her hand and led her upstairs to her bedroom. They sat in silence, side by side, on the bed. Esther was still wearing her coat and she wrapped it round herself, suddenly conscious of how short her dress was. She must have looked a mess, her eyeliner smudged and her mouth red raw from kissing Alesha all night. There was a beansprout on her sleeve, she noticed, and picked it off, remembering how much she and Alesha had laughed as they fought over the bits of beef in the chow mein they'd shared on the bus home. Esther could still feel the heat of the foil tray in her palm.

"When did he die?" she asked, toes curling into the pink carpet.

"Christmas Eve."

"That was a week ago." Esther frowned and Sam shrugged. "How?"

"Cancer," Sam said, staring at the Gordon Parks poster on the opposite wall.

The word struck her like a punch. She didn't know what to say, so just said, "Shit."

"I know."

"Was it sudden?"

Sam shook her head.

"How long have you known?"

"Ages."

"Is that why you were in Cyprus all summer?"

Sam nodded. "He wanted to go home one last time."

"Shit." Esther rubbed her forehead with her hand. "Why didn't you tell me?"

"He didn't want anyone to know."

I'm not anyone, Esther almost said but bit her tongue so hard she tasted blood.

"You OK?" she asked instead and immediately regretted it, looking down at the blisters on her bare feet. Of course she wasn't OK. "Can I get you anything? Do you want a cup of tea or something?" Esther immediately regretted saying that as well. Her father had just died. How was tea going to help?

"I just…" Sam stopped to wipe away a tear with her fingers then started again. "I just need you to be you."

•

An hour later they were curled up like a couple of commas on the narrow single bed. Esther was still in her coat and Sam was still in her DMs, the pair of them lying in silence on top of the sheets.

"I'm sorry," Sam said into the dark when she thought Esther was asleep.

But she wasn't. And she wasn't asleep a few hours later when Sam untangled herself and slipped out of the room.

•

No doubt you're wondering why I didn't intervene but before you question my motives, let me say this: what's meant for you won't pass you by, I promise you that.

So I let it play out.

You probably think I shouldn't have – but I knew that Esther kept going back to Sam because she felt like home and Sam kept going back to Esther because she tasted like home, like summer and Christmas and the birthday cake she had on her thirteenth birthday, like the last time she was truly happy. But you can't make another person home. I know that and you know that but Esther didn't, so I had to wait. Wait until the next morning – the fateful New Year's Eve I told you about – when she asked Alesha to meet her in that bookshop in Haggerston. I knew what she was going to do and I almost stopped her. But I had faith in sweet Esther, just like you should have faith in me, so I let her do it. She almost didn't because she knew Alesha would never look at her like that again, like she was the only thing she could see for miles.

Miles and miles.

But she did.

"This isn't working," she said, the words so hard to

say she almost broke her teeth on them.

Alesha looked genuinely confused. "What isn't working? Do you want to go somewhere else?"

"No. *This* isn't working. You and me."

There was a long moment of silence as Alesha stared at her, the skin between her thin eyebrows pinched. Eventually she sat back and tilted her head at Esther. "Are you breaking up with me?"

Esther nodded.

"Why, Ess?"

"It isn't working."

"Why?"

Stop asking me why, Esther wanted to yell. She reached for her coffee.

"Is this something to do with that girl?" Alesha said suddenly, and Esther put down the mug and looked her in the eye for the first time since she'd walked into the bookshop.

"What girl?"

"The one who was waiting outside your house last night."

Esther's heart threw itself against her ribs. "You saw her?"

"I know you're too scared to let me walk you all the way home in case your parents see but I always wait at the top of your road to make sure you get in OK."

Esther's whole face burned.

"Who is she, Ess?"

"No one," she said too quickly and Alesha shook her head at her.

"You're lying."

"No."

"Why are you lying, Ess?"

"I'm not."

"Who is she, then?"

"My best friend."

"You've never mentioned a best friend."

"Haven't I?" Esther said, picking an imaginary piece of fluff off her jeans.

"Why was she waiting for you outside your house at midnight?"

"Her dad died." As soon as the words were out of her mouth, Esther cursed herself.

What was she doing playing the dead dad card? Was she trying to shame Alesha into believing her?

It didn't work.

"So why lie, Ess?"

"I didn't."

"You did. You said she was no one."

"I meant no one like *that*."

"Like what?"

"I didn't want you to get the wrong idea."

"Why would I get the wrong idea?"

Esther's hands balled into fists in her lap. "You're twisting my words."

"I'm just asking why you think I'd get the wrong idea about you talking to your best friend about her dad dying? Unless she's more than a friend, of course." When Esther pushed the coffee cup away from her, Alesha sat back and sighed tenderly. "You shagged her, didn't you?"

"Of course not!" Esther raised her voice and everyone in the bookshop turned to look but she didn't care, wiping her nose with the sleeve of her hoodie. "Don't turn it into that. It's not like that."

"Like what?"

"You wouldn't understand."

"Help me understand, then."

"I've loved her my whole life. I don't even know how

to love someone else."

"So you're not even going to try?"

"She's the only person I've ever loved, Alesha."

No, she was the first person she'd ever loved, there's a difference. But she didn't know that. The sad thing was that she thought it was what Sam needed. The truth was: Sam needed a friend but that was all she needed. She just didn't know how to tell Esther that.

"So what now?" Alesha pushed.

"I don't know."

"You must know because you're dumping me." Esther turned her head but Alesha didn't let her get away with it. "So are you going to be with her, then?"

"I don't know."

"Stop saying that you don't know."

"Stop asking me questions I can't answer, then."

They glared at one another across the small table. Esther looked away first.

"So that's it?" Alesha asked.

"I guess."

"You guess? You're ending this for 'I guess'?" Esther couldn't look at her, but Alesha kept pushing. "So are you going to be with her or not?"

"Probably not."

"Probably not? You mean, you don't even know?"

"You don't know Sam," Esther said under her breath.

"No, I don't know Sam, but I thought I knew you."

Esther's cheeks burned.

"So what?" Alesha shrugged. "Are you waiting for me to make the big speech? Pick me. Please, pick me."

"Of course not."

"I'm not going to beg, Ess."

"I'm not asking you to."

"What, then?"

"I don't know."

Alesha closed her eyes and held up her hand. "Ess, if you say 'I don't know' one more time, I swear…"

When she opened them again, all Esther could do was shrug. "What do you want me to say?"

"I want you to say that you haven't been fucking me around for four months." Her voice cracked as she said it and it hurt Esther so much to hear that it felt like every one of her bones broke at once. "I want you to say that you don't choose her, you choose me." Alesha smacked her chest with her hand. "I want you to pick me."

Esther knew then what she'd done. I had given her two choices: Sam, the only person she'd ever loved but who couldn't love her back, at least not in the way Esther wanted her to, or Alesha, who did love her back – all of her, in every way she knew how – without Esther having to change a thing about herself.

She had two choices and she chose wrong.

Don't be too hard on her, though. You must remember what it was like to be stupid and scared and sixteen. Perhaps you're still stupid and scared and sixteen. As soon as she realized what she'd done, Esther wanted to take it all back, to snatch up the words with her hands, stuff them back into her mouth and swallow them. But Alesha was looking at her, her eyes wet and her chin quivering, so when she parted her lips, nothing came out.

"Well." Alesha snatched her phone off the table and stood up. "There you go."

The bell rang over the door as she walked out. At that point I wanted to kick Esther, but I didn't have to. She was already out of her chair. The bell rang again as she ran into the street and Alesha must have heard because she stopped and turned to look at her, hands in her coat pockets.

Say it, Alesha thought.

Say it, I thought.

"Of course it's you," Esther said.

That's when the magic happened. The stars aligned and the earth shifted. Esther took a step forwards and Alesha took one, the pair of them meeting in the middle in a kiss that might not make the history books but it made them weak. Call it what you like but all I did was get them to the same place at the same time.

The rest was up to them.

WE WHO?

·

Nikesh Shukla

I write in silence most nights. Once I've shut down YouTube and Tumblr and I'm not listening to Solange on repeat any more. It's just me and the white glow of Dad's laptop in my dark bedroom. The only sounds are the laptop's fan working overtime and, every now and then, drunken students stumbling home to the halls at the end of our road. The quiet helps me focus. That's when I get my best writing done, scribbling couplets that would make Little Simz proud.

I once saw her.

Alex and I were at a gig and she was in the crowd. She was chatting to her mates like they were the most normal people in the world and I wanted to be in that chat so much. I don't know what they were jibber-jabbering about and I don't know what I would have contributed given I'm mostly mute in social situations, but to stand there and have a normal conversation with such an icon, that would be a dream. Why can I write down everything I want to say, but never just say it out loud?

Alex kept saying, "Go chat to her, go chat to her." But I couldn't do it. I just stood there, staring. Alex offered me a tap on the shoulder as a way of saying never mind and we turned our heads back to the stage.

Sometimes I think back to that moment and fantasize about going up to her, and I wonder what life would be like if I'd done it.

Tonight I'm not writing. I need to find that happy place, where I dream that I'm approaching Little Simz and her mates like I'm part of the gang, instead of just standing there like I did in real life. I'm walking away from Alex.

Because Alex has just shared a Britain First video on their Facebook. Their comment alongside it is two emojis: a Union Jack flag and a white thumbs up.

Two weeks ago Alex told me their dad voted Leave. It came up because I had posted a #tbt to the day of the referendum. I'd been volunteering for the Remain campaign. The photo is of the Stronger In badge on my hoodie. I wrote underneath the gram: "Not all Leave voters are racist, but they are standing by and let racists hijack their vote. Silence is complicity." It was something Mum said to me when we were walking back from the shops, two packets of cold paneer getting sweaty in my hands as we strolled. Every now and then, she had to stop and listen to people complain about bins, about drug users in the park, about how this country was being overrun by immigrants and there were no opportunities for good honest working folk. It pains me I'm not old enough to vote and it pains me that the votes of the young didn't count more than the votes of the old. How can you vote for something that'll happen after you die? You legit have no horse in the race. Every single time Mum got given a hard time, especially about immigrants, it was from old people. I asked her how she managed to face such hate.

"You need to understand the power of being listened to," she told me.

I understand that already. I spend most of my time listening. I wasn't always shy. But moving from that tiny school to this big one, it whipped away any confidence I had.

Almost immediately after I posted that #tbt, Alex messaged me and asked if we could chat. I called their phone. Crying, they told me they were ashamed of their dad. He had voted Leave, and he had done so because he was sick of this country being overrun by immigrants.

Alex said they felt like they had to tell me, given how often I was over at their yard. They felt bad that they'd been holding on to the secret since it happened.

"Whenever you're over and I see you joking with him," Alex said. "Do you know how hard that is, knowing what I know?"

I sat in silence, listening, not sure what to think. I loved Alex and Alex's family. We'd been friends since primary school, inseparable. We did homework together, we wrote poetry together, we spent most of every evening watching the same shows on television and WhatsApping a running commentary back and forth. Alex was an indelible part of my life. I went to their house every Christmas Eve.

"Your dad wants me deported?" I mumbled.

"Did you know," Alex told me, "there's a convicted rapist from Romania living in the UK, on benefits, and because of European statutes, we can't send him back to where he came from."

"Would you prefer rapists to be good ol'-fashioned British ones?" I said.

We fell into an awkward silence. I could hear them breathing. I held my breath.

"My dad's not a racist," Alex told me. "He's my dad."

There was this moment where neither of us spoke, where everything in the room seemed to be humming. I wanted to tell Alex that what their dad thought wasn't a reflection on them. I was desperate for things to go back to us joking about something or other and not this tense atmosphere on the phone. I could feel my stomach churning over and over.

"Can I send you a new poem for some feedback?" Alex asked, almost like the entire exchange before hadn't happened.

"Sure," I said.

I didn't think any more about the conversation but, on reflection, I can see that Alex pulled back. We WhatsApped all the time still but the running commentary just slipped into the occasional emoji. I kept asking if they were OK and Alex kept telling me everything was fine. I got more and more invested in finishing this collection of poems I was working on, inspired by the songs of Bessie Smith. I sent them over to Alex, as I always did, and Alex sent them back with notes, but the notes became more sporadic, less in-depth. They stopped sending me poems they wrote or YouTube videos of songs they liked or daily writing tips

•

All of the last few weeks pass through my mind as the video plays, silently, in my feed. Curious to know what Alex has shared, I reload the video, switch the volume on and watch.

There's a man in a balaclava, standing in front of a brick wall. There is the ambient clink of glasses and chatter of people you can't see in the background. It's probably been shot in a pub car park next to some bins or something.

The man talks about it being time to reclaim Britain from the Islamist scum.

He talks quickly, breathlessly, like he's about to be shut down. "In recent months, our group has grown. Membership is swelling by the tens of thousands.

There are battalions everywhere, in every locale, in every town, village, major city. And we are gaining more and more attention on Facebook. We've got more likes than UKIP now. And we are headed for war. The politicians don't care about us so we have to take our message to the streets of England. Remind the indigenous population of the white genocide going on around them. The eradication of the white race, by Britain being turned into a Muslim ghetto. They call me a racist. I'm just concerned about my country."

The video ends, and I sit staring at the end screen in silence.

Alex shared this.

We've known each other since primary school. Alex moved in with us when their dad had his hip replacement. We wrote a collection of anti-war poems together.

This is a betrayal.

I go to bed but I don't sleep. My brain whirrs, thinking about what I'll say to Alex tomorrow at school, but the more I try and create scenarios where I confront Alex, the more elaborate their responses become. After a while my phone stops lighting up with notifications so it must be late. I should be asleep.

At 4.37 a.m. I sit up and press space bar on the laptop. It whirrs loudly to life.

I press refresh on Alex's page. The post is still there.

I type, WTF?

A minute later, I delete my comment and close the laptop.

•

Mum and I are doing the weekly shop. Well, she's doing the weekly shop. I'm on my phone and pulling a trolley behind me as we navigate the tight aisles of Sweet Mart. She picks through okra until she finds the best ones, puts them in a plastic bag and tosses it to me to put in the trolley. I'm scrolling through Tumblr, reblogging a slew of reports of hate-crime incidents in the city, including CCTV and phone footage. I don't have that many followers but it makes me feel like I'm doing something, even if I'm caning my data.

"Get off your phone," Mum says. "It's mango season."

She gestures to a box – '5 for £5'. I shrug. "I don't like mangos."

"Yes, you do," she replies, laughing.

"I don't. You just always think I do…"

"I do not understand anyone who doesn't like mango. It's impossible to not like mango. Mango is the fruit of the gods."

"No, Mum," I say. "It's stringy and the texture and taste don't match."

I return to my phone.

We walk down the aisle and she stops and turns to me.

"Would you like to talk to me about anything?" she asks.

"No," I say. "I'm fine."

"Just because my job requires me to listen to the entire borough's problems," she says, "it doesn't mean I won't have time to listen to yours. Yours are the most important."

"I'm OK."

•

In the car, we're listening to Bessie Smith, my mum's favourite. She is singing about how you won't be the same so see if I care.

The words seem to be catering specifically to me today.

"Mum," I say, turning to her. "How do you deal with people who have different opinions to you?"

"By remembering that they are not my friends."

"What if one of them is your friend?"

Mum flicks a look over to me. "You and your friends won't always believe the same things. Difference is important. Having different views on life isn't the worst thing in the world. It keeps things interesting."

"What if the thing they believe is hurtful and hateful?"

"How we define hate and hurt is what makes us human," Mum says elusively, like she's dodging my question. "You can tell a lot about a person from how much tolerance they show to people they disagree with. Believing in freedom of thought and opinion is the only way to live."

"But I don't understand how I'm supposed to try and empathize with someone who doesn't view *me* as human."

"Darling," my mum says, "no one said anything about empathy. If people want the freedom to say and think what they want, you have the freedom to challenge them. It's your duty."

I turn to face the window so Mum can't see me cry.

I feel alone. I know I need to tell my best friend that sharing that video is a betrayal. It's hurtful. And it is pretty much a deal-breaker for our friendship. Especially if that's what they think of my family. That we are ruining the country.

•

Alex approaches me at the bus stop. I'm sitting down, headphones on and looking at the way the red swoosh on my trainers makes the white background really stand out. It feels empowering. Last night I reblogged this quote from Zora Neale Hurston, one of my English teacher's favourite authors. "I feel most coloured when I am thrown against a sharp white background". That's how I feel today. I can see Alex hovering in my periphery. They are listening to a conversation Jay and Kiran are having, all the while glancing over to look at me. There's nothing playing on my headphones. They're there as a barrier.

Alex walks over, arms folded and stands in front of me expectantly as I slowly take off my headphones.

"You going to Paul's party later?" they ask, almost aggressively.

"Nah," I say. "Staying in, innit."

"Writing?" comes the reply, and in that brief single word, we feel normal again. I nod. "OK, then, that's good," they add before turning round, sighing audibly and walking back towards Jay and Kiran. Jay has waved goodbye, to walk off to her sixth form. Alex waves at her, looking at me the entire time. They say something to Kiran and they both laugh. I want to walk over and join them and laugh, too, like I'm one of the gang. I'm back in that moment, at that gig, on the outside, watching Little Simz and her mates crack jokes. And I'm standing back. It almost doesn't matter how betrayed I feel by Alex. I just want to be laughing with them like everything is normal. I put my headphones back on. No music, but the barrier is enough to tune out the world.

•

When the bus arrives, I'm one of the slowest to move, which makes me the last to get on. I spot a seat next to Alex. It's the only one available. Even though we haven't talked about the thing between us, we can both feel it there, like the last slice of pizza. You both wait the other out, hoping for them to either just grab for the pizza or leave the table so you can stuff it in your face.

I sit next to Alex but I keep my headphones on.

I can feel them bristle, placing their cheek against the window. The condensation must be making their whole cheek wet.

I remember one of the first days we met. At school. Bonding over matching Spider-Man lunchboxes, marvelling at how different the contents were. I'd never eaten a sandwich before. Alex had never had a samosa. So we swapped. They spat out the samosa because it was too spicy. The sandwich was all gakky and mulchy in my mouth and I managed two bites before passing it back.

We laughed about it once Alex had drunk their bodyweight in water and I had finished the samosa, just to get rid of the taste of the sliced white bread.

"What is that?" I asked.

"A sandwich. It's the most English thing in the world."

"It's like eating a sponge."

"The samosa burned my mouth."

"I know. It's delicious."

We laughed over our difference then spent years bonding over things that made us the same. I don't want that any more.

I nod my head to some imaginary music, to continue the illusion we're ignoring each other. I know I need to take off my headphones, turn to Alex and tell them what that Britain First video did to me.

But I can't bring myself to do it. Because this isn't about their dad or the political atmosphere of the country or whether they even believe it. It's about whether our friendship is worth salvaging. Do I want it to be?

Later that day, Alex doesn't sit next to me in English like they usually do. I pretend not to notice.

•

That night, Alex posts on Tumblr:

<<<<THESE GUYS ARE SPEAKING BARE TRUTHS YOU KNOW>>>>

It's a comment underneath an image they're reblogging. The image is of some friends in a circle, looking intense, arms around each other in solidarity. One of them wears a WHITE GENOCIDE T-shirt. The first sentence of the post is about how multiculturalism is killing the white race. I don't want to read any more.

The night feels heavy after that, laden with memories I second-guess. When Alex said this, did they really mean this? When I was here and this happened and Alex said it was fine, was it really fine? It's like I've been looking at my best friend through glasses that make us the same rather than seeing all the things that make us different. Neither should be cause for friction. Still, I'm starting to wonder whether my friend is even my friend. It doesn't make sense.

Minutes later, Alex posts up a photo of a placard. It says ALL LIVES MATTER.

I post up a poem that Alex and I wrote together, a year ago. It's about two friends who fall out about something stupid and the chasm between them grows till neither can remember what triggered the argument. The poem ends, twenty years later, as they pass each other in the street and neither can remember who the other is.

Alex likes the post. And in the comments, posts: 'Clear Eyes, Full Heart, Can't Lose'.

The amount of time we've spent talking about *Friday*

Night Lights, it could fill a book. I just don't want to believe that my friend could post these things and still call themselves my friend.

Maybe therein lies the problem.

●

I see Alex alone the next day and sit down next to them on the bench. I feel them shift into the corner, squirming to be as far away from me as possible. There's this churn in my stomach because there is so much unsaid between Alex and me and that is not the natural order of things in our lives.

I don't want to do this. I look out on to the 'hangout' zone that stretches between the two college buildings. People are hanging out. Watching videos on phones, chatting, a guy strumming his guitar in the corner with his eyes closed, definitely not doing it for attention.

"Yes?" Alex says.

"Can we talk?"

"About?"

"What's going on," I ask. "Between you and me."

"Whatever," they say, quiet.

"Alex, why do you keep sharing that racist shit on the internet?"

"I'm sorry if you find it offensive."

"It's not just me. I know you don't believe all that 'white genocide, all lives matter' crap. You're better than that."

Alex turns to me. For a second, they look like a stranger.

"Am I? Or am I just a dumb white person?"

"What?"

"I know what your sort think. You think that all white people are racist."

"I never said that," I reply. "What are you talking about?"

"Look, I've just been reading up about a lot of things online and I feel like my race is being picked on. We were here first."

"Is this about your dad?" I ask.

Alex turns to look at me, tears streaming down their face. They sit up.

"Don't talk about him," Alex says, sighing slowly.

"Alex, we're friends. Best friends."

"If you can't be in the same room as him, you can't

be in the same room as me. We're the same."

"Alex, this isn't helpful. Your dad is your dad. You're you. We can still be friends."

"I don't even understand how you can be like that with him. He doesn't hate all immigrants. He thinks you're all right. You were born here. You're English. It's the ones who are straining the NHS, the ones taking jobs – you know Simon hasn't been able to find a job in six months? You know why?"

"Cos he smokes all that weed?" I say, hoping a joke we both share will bring us back together.

"Immigrants."

To hear my best friend aping the words of their dad without questioning them, I feel destroyed and everything unravels.

Maybe once we add context to memory it gives it a nuance we miss first-time round. Maybe when Alex rejected that samosa. Maybe when Alex's dad told me he hoped my mum wasn't planning to join ISIS because she'd visited a mosque. Maybe when Alex's mum smiles and asks if I eat bacon because who knows what's offensive any more. Maybe the casual build-up of hatred from leaving a stack of

*Daily Mail*s next to the downstairs download. Maybe all these things and nothing. Maybe an actual reason and maybe the victim of easy influence. Maybe all of these things and none of them.

"Alex," I tell my supposed best friend. "I don't know who is talking right now, you or your dad, but if you are making decisions about people because of wh—"

"Don't you get it?" Alex shouts. "It isn't you. We're not talking about you. We're talking about them."

"No, Alex," I say firmly. "You're talking about us. I am them."

"We're not the same as them," Alex says angrily.

"We who?" I ask, and the question hangs as a bell goes off, telling us lunch is over.

We both sit there, frozen to the seat. I look out at the trees at the end of the car park and wonder what's beyond them.

We who, I ask myself. *We who?*

THE CLEAN SWEEP

·

Patrice Lawrence

OK, Ruby. I ain't making excuses, but it was Emo's idea. The whole damn thing was his. He called it the Making Out For Lost Time Plan. We're supposed to lips as many girls as we can in the forty-eight hours left. Just as well you can't see me. My ears are burning telling you this.

There were always going to be problems with this great idea of his. Number One, there's the girl to boy ratio. One of them to every ten of us. And the girls that *are* here, you have to approach them with caution. These girls are the tough ones. They call them the nation's worst. Number Two, there's good reasons why me and Emo never score in the first place. We see them every time we look in the mirror. And the fact our world's going to end in two days' time hasn't jacked up our chances.

So far, Emo's managed the mighty sum of ... one girl. She's called Daphne. They're here on the beach, folded into each other, curled up inside an old deckchair frame like they want to be in a picture. They've laid down a blanket but these pebbles are cold, man. That takes serious dedication.

And me, well... I'm not saying I'm hideous, Ruby. That ain't fair on you. And maybe some day you'll find a picture of me to prove it. But I'm just gonna say that even with one girl, Emo's a good stage ahead in his plan than me. My lips are still lonely.

Before I go on, I'll give you a visual. I should have got the cam on this thing fixed when I had a chance. But then I should have done loads of stuff when I had a chance. And there's loads more stuff I shouldn't have done. Now's not the time to make *that* list. It would fill up all the minutes.

So where am I? Like I said, I'm on the beach and it's bone cold. The sea's sludge and the sky's kind of frowning. The clouds are creased up and wrinkly. The sun's dripping dirty light, like it got washed in the sea first. The dark's on its way. I can see it dragging itself over the bashed-up hotels and chip shops on the Parade.

In two days' time, they'll all be gone. All of us lot, too. It's hard to get my head round it.

These last few days, the beach has got busy. Everyone's huddled in pairs, like they're waiting for an ark. But when the Clean Sweep comes, we're all going out – one by one.

Sound: Background voices. Words inaudible.

Silence: 11 seconds.

Emo's stuck his oar in. He's unhooked his mouth from Daphne's to tell me I should take this conversation wider. He said I'm making it sound like we're a load of teenagers having a night-time grope on the beach. Or not having a grope, in my case. He said, I should set the scene properly. He's right, Ruby. This is my last chance to tell you who I am.

We're in Youth Reform. All of us are. I've seen a few behaviour realignment camps in my time, but this was meant to be something new. That's what they told us, Ruby. If we were proper serious about wanting to change, this was our last chance. Realignment don't come cheap and the politicians are pulling the funds. After the last thing I did, that thing … I wasn't sent to one of the usual institutions. I was told I'd been selected – selected, Ruby – for this new kind of therapy. They were bigging it up, like I should be grateful to be their guinea pig. I was gonna refuse, but then they gave me a picture of you. It's my only one. That's what made me sign on the dotted line.

Man, when we got off the security vans and saw we'd landed here, we had to laugh. All those politicians keep moaning that prison's a holiday camp, that all them hard-working families are paying extras to keep us off the street when their kids don't get no treats. And now it looked like every axe-wielding young psycho, every junior arsonist and apprentice head-smasher had got themselves a free pass to the seaside. They even gave us giant lollipops and filmed us as we went through the gates. Clever, right, Ruby? Those hard-working families could hate us even more.

And they had plenty more chances. Soon as they let us loose in here, we saw there were cameras everywhere. Yeah, all prisons have them, but this was more. They fixed up a rig round the Dome roof and had a camera whirling round it 24/7. Trip wires looped backwards and forwards between those little shops in the Lanes so cameras could whizz over our heads when we went those ways. Not that we had much need to. None of the shops were open; some of them were proper boarded up with metal doors and shutters. Emo reckons there were tech crews in there, but I never saw anyone come or go. There was a sweet shop and the trainer shop, though. Closed down, but you could see the stock through the window. By the end of the first day, it was just broken glass and empty shelves. All of it live-streamed to the great world beyond.

Maybe you'll find the footage, Ruby. Don't worry, I'm not in it. I don't need Air Max nor humbugs.

We got our own cam and mic, too, to record our 'inspirational journeys'. Some of us got extra privileges if we let them use our journeys for 'educational' purposes. Lots of nice little clips with music behind them that they could show between the riots, because the public need someone to like. Too much hating's gonna make them turn off.

Hang on. There's something I want you to hear. I'll shut up so you can listen.

I'm holding the mic up.

Get it? It's the humming sound. Listen again.

Sound: Analysis suggests the engine of a low-flying

aircraft, possibly an automated unmanned vehicle. No substantive evidence available to confirm.

I suppose it doesn't mean anything to you. But us! Man, it's hooked into a deep part of our brain. It's been thirty days and we still look up. It's a black shadow with flickering green lights across the undercarriage. A number and a word. The number's the countdown, days left until it's all over. The word – it's supposed to be YES or NO. The numbers change. But ever since the countdown started, the word stays the same.

YES.

I don't know the exact question, Ruby. I hope you can find that out. But whatever it was, all the citizens of the world, nosing through the livestream, having a quick gulp from our lives, most of them voted 'yes'.

'Do you want to see that scum wiped from the face of the earth?'

You got TWO days left to change your mind. What do you think?

YES.

The plane's dead still. I want it to drop into the sea. I want the engines to flood. I want the lights to fizz out. I want time to stop.

It's moving away, taking its time, making sure everyone gets a good look.

We came here in three loads, fifty each time over a month. And maybe that was part of the experiment. Seeing how we would all get on. Survival of the fittest and all that. Take 150 maniacs and dump them in a falling-down town with just enough food. Film all the tough stuff, the blood, the stretchers, the helicopters landing. Stick it on the internet and add adverts.

'Your teenager turning into a violent little git? All that bone-breaking's making him a bit peckish? Why not try Squeejee's Chocolate Ketchup on his bacon sandwich?'

The lot who set this up needed all that money. The Prison Institute is loaded but it's not gonna risk its dosh on something like this. This kinda experiment ain't coming cheap. There's a giant wall with all the wire and cameras you'll ever need keeping us in on land side. Catcher nets and guard boats in the shallows between the pier ruins. Spy drones going over, too, or maybe they're the cameras, for those essential overhead views. You don't wanna miss that special shot of Mad Jill slamming Josh's nose against the boat-shed door.

Emo reckons there was whole wads of money shoved in the bigwigs' sweaty hands, too, because how else you gonna sort the ethics?

Though they've got the public on their side. According to them, we don't deserve no ethics.

Sorry, Ruby, I'm sounding a bit sharp now. That's why I'm Ritchie-No-Mates. No girl's gonna lips me in case her mouth gets scarred with the acid.

Most of the hotels here are on the tumble. There's masses of tunnels under the town, hundreds of people over hundreds of years, all trying to bury their secrets. The salt's eating the foundations and the buildings are crumbling in. The ones still standing were turned into voluntary therapy units. We were told it was up to us to check ourselves in to sort out our problems. There were do-gooders everywhere. (Though take my advice, Ruby. Don't you ever use that word!) Even if you went for a battered sausage in the chip shop and it was a youth worker who was going to serve it to you. And a counsellor unscrewing the pickled eggs. They set up schools in the Pavilion and the Dome. Everything from looking after horses to catching up on your algorithms.

The thing was, you didn't have to go. And who went? Someone did, because when the youthies and the therapists disappeared, a load of kids went with them. But maybe they were just the extras all along, setting the scene.

After that, the public got to vote if we should remain. A thirty-day countdown. Me and Emo tried to imagine what was going on outside the wall, if anyone was arguing for us. If they were, they were really bad at it.

'Do you think they've used up all their chances?'

YES.

Emo and Daphne are talking. I can't hear the words. If you can, the mic on this thing's better than I thought. Emo's arms reaching out, gentle so he doesn't disturb her and his fingers are next to mine. I've just turned away so Daphne can't hear me say this, but that's our sign. Little fingers hooked together. The Making Out For Lost Time Plan's dead. He's telling me he understands there's something else I need to do.

Sound: Double click. Tech analysis suggests audio terminated and rebooted. Automated time-code metrics recorded 17 minutes 43 seconds void time.

•

I'm not on the beach no more. Hear that whistling sound? It's the wind. It's always worse up on the Parade, knifing it through you. The moon's out now, big and pale like my nan's face when she has toothache. There's a bench next to me with a load of names gouged into the wood. Rav and Rosie, Whitehawk Warriors, Black Regents. I can see dots of light from the candles up and down the shoreline and the shell of the Palace Pier. The helter skelter's still there, like it's giving us the finger.

There's a giant bonfire in the old mall. I can smell it crackling in the air. Must be the junior arsonists' final meet-up. I heard they drained the oil out the chip fryers and buried bottles of it in the middle of the old sofas and mannequins. They're gonna make sure we go out with a bang.

The Grand Hotel's right behind me. I have to remember it's just broken windows, smashed-up walls and splinters now. The guards are gone. And the floodlights. And the realignment rooms.

There's still cameras on top of the poles in front,

moving side to side, like flags in the wind. I hope they got my good side, the not-hideous angle. The Grand's still got the solar, though the lights have turned sick blue. So I'm probably gonna look like I just come out a frozen-food cabinet.

I'm moving closer. Glass is crunching under my feet. Can you hear it?

This place. This place, Ruby. One thing I'm gonna hope is that they don't have places like this where you are. No one was going to share the feed from in here. Though the light was so bright in my room, it was like they were planning a twenty-four-hour film shoot. Never turned off. Never night. I'd be sitting on the floor, my back against the door so long, I think my shape must have got sweated into the wood.

And Ruby, the thing that got me through it was you.

A week after voluntary therapy ended, they landed helicopters by the Pavilion. There were so many of them, we thought 'Experiment terminated! We're going home!' But when they opened the doors, it was proper thug-boy stormtroopers. Emo and me were in the crowd watching, when suddenly one of them turned to look at us. First thing we noticed was that his gun was so big that if he pulled the trigger, the bullet was going straight through us, across the Channel and into some poor kid in France. The second thing we noticed was that every one of them had a minicam in a cage on top of their helmet. A proper live broadcast special.

They cordoned off the Grand and cleared it out. Every single machine – the brain-zappers, the scanners, even the metal trolleys for the hardcore meds. All the quacks and shrinks and youthies had gone before. We hadn't realized that. Come to think of it, we didn't see any of them leave. They probably drugged us all up and smuggled them out one night.

Anyway, time for another visual. I'm still outside, near where the posh people used to have their breakfast, a long glass room to munch their toast. It was way before the no-boat zone, so they'd see the ferries and the cruisers and the fisherboats. And maybe at nights when they sipped their soup and champagne, they watched the bright lights running up and down the pier.

We got soup, too. But most of us were so zapped, we needed help to feed. That's how me and Emo met, trying to spoon leek and potato through each other's wobbly lips. You have to stay friends after something like that.

When the stormtroopers blasted off and we were sure no one was coming back, this place got a proper bash-up. I wanted to join in. I came with a brick in one hand and a piece of pipe in the other. Emo found an old hammer head on the beach. But we got to where I'm standing now and I could taste old blood in my mouth and my back pulled tight and … Ruby, my body forgot the basic things. Like breathing. Like making my heart slow down so the blood could catch up. Like how boys like me don't just stand there and cry.

I looked at Emo and he looked at me and we dropped our tools and walked away. Neither of us have been back since.

Jesus, man! I'm staring at the smashed-out windows and there was something…

Shit!

Background noise: 22 seconds. Analysis implies crushed broken glass. Not verified.

There was something against my ankle. My breath, man. So loud it sounds like shouting. That's how this place still makes me. OK. OK. Calming down.

I know they've got rats here and rats don't bother me. They're just keeping themselves to themselves, chilling until they take the town over in two days' time. They don't care about the Clean Sweep. They're gonna survive. Them and the cockroaches.

Shit! It happened again! Shit!

Ruby, girl, you're gonna feel proper shame. I looked down ready to see a scaly tail twisting through the glass splinters but it's a cat – not much more than a kitten. Its fur's full of ash and dust, and the light's making it glow like a ghost. It shouldn't be here. Its paws must be cut to shreds.

It butted me again. You hear the meow? A little thing like that shouldn't make a sound so big.

Now it's gone back into the hotel, bold as a bad man. I just need to follow it. I just need to walk straight through the hole where the door is, along the corridor and up the stairs.

Period of on/off time: Unverifiable.

•

I've done it! I'm inside!

And you know how I managed it? I thought of the

Clean Sweep! The water's gonna be as high as a house, flushing out all the crap and every trace of us. A giant wave, breaking through the tiles and bricks, killing our fires and dragging everything back out with it. They've calculated it exactly, they said, how much bomb to drop from how high up and how far out. And the Sweep's gonna take the Grand, too. It's nothing but a building.

All I have to do now is go up two flights of stairs and find my old realignment room. It was next to the lift. I know that because I spent all night hearing it go up and down, waiting for my door to open, the blindfold to slip over my head.

OK. I'm in. I'm going to try and tell you what it's like inside. I hope you can hear me because I'm whispering. I'm like those people in TV nature documentaries walking through night jungles, not sure what's around me, don't want to disturb nothing bad. The guard lights in the old reception area are blinking. Solar must be nearly drained. There's a hallway at the end.

The lights are flickering now, shaking in time with me. When they blink off, it's a tunnel of black. That's where I'm heading.

Background noise: 13 seconds. Analysis indicates crushed broken glass. Not verified.

I'm in the hallway. My back's against the wall and I'm sliding along. I'm reaching my hand out in front of me, like I'm trying to catch the dark. My fingers are flashing on and off washy blue. There's bumps and grooves and sharp things under my boots. Something's run over my foot, but I haven't coughed up my heart this time because I know it's the cat. Or its identical twin. It's just hightailed it into a side room.

The lights are really troubled. I need to find the staircase quick. Blue flash. Then dark. I'm whispering even quieter but it feels like the walls are yelling my words back. I can feel plaster cracks, wallpaper flakes, and there's a gritty hole, maybe an old electricity socket. And the Grand is humming, like it's having a big think.

Do you hear it? Please, Ruby, I hope you hear it and it's not just me going mad.

The solar's dead now. It's proper dark, so thick I can wear it. I could drop my trews, pull off my shirt and my socks and roll around in it. I don't mean to laugh but I can't help it.

Sorry. Sorry. I'll try and get it together.

But the humming's started again. There's words in the humming, a thin voice, fading in and out. It's the voice of bones.

Please, please hear it.

Sound analysis: 'Humming' identified as low-energy warning.

Voice analysis: Female, age indication 14 to 17 years old. Words inaudible.

The dark's shifting around me. It's crawling out of the walls. But I found the stairs. It's all right. They're here. They're here. But there's spots of lights coming towards me. And behind that, deeper dark. It's moving, too. And—

Sound: Non-human suggestive of sudden pain.

Sound: Bang. Estimated 117 decibels.

Sound: Double click. Tech analysis suggests audio terminated and rebooted. Automated time-code metrics recorded 10 hours, 33 minutes 09 seconds void time.

●

I want to open my eyes but, man, everything hurts. Even my eyelids. It feels like if I try and lift them, they're going to rip the skin off the rest of my face. So I'm going to wait a few more seconds.

I'm lying on something hard and flat. I tripped over the bloody cat and must have banged my head on the stairs.

My head… It's like when they brought me back from compulsory therapy. It feels like a drone's tried to land in it. No. I won't go backwards to that time. But what if I've gone forwards? What if I've slept forty-eight hours! What if it's today? What if everything's already decided? The big, final YES.

What if there's no more time and we've got to ZERO?

Right. I've done it. I've opened my eyes. The ceiling's cracked and stained brown. Bunches of wires are poking out the holes and some of the walls, too. I'm trying to sit up, but my head feels like it's been twisted off and put back on wrong.

There's something… Someone? Bending over me. She's holding a…

Sound: Double click. Tech analysis suggests audio terminated and rebooted. Automated time-code metrics recorded 8 hours, 0 minutes 17 seconds void time.

•

Two words, Ruby. YES. And ONE.

The plane's circling back round and coming over again. But ONE plus a second ONE don't make TWO. There's just ONE day left.

I've been quiet for a while but my audio was down to eight per cent. I'll bring you up to date. I'm with Maria.

When I came round this morning, I was lying on a low table. Suddenly this face loomed up over me. I tried to sit up too quickly and the table tipped up and dumped me on the stinking squelch of carpet. Then the damn thing landed on top of me, banging me hard in my face. I'm surprised my teeth stayed stuck in my head.

There I was, scrabbling like a rat on its back, when the table was lifted off. It was hard to see who was doing it because the face was too close up to fit in my brain in one piece. I saw an eye. It was dark with long eyelashes. Then brown skin and a little C shape of spots across the forehead. (Sorry, I had to whisper that bit.)

A sharp point dug into the skin under my ribs.

"You're not trying nothing, right?"

I tried to shake my head but my face felt like it was going to splatter from the inside out. And then I saw what was in her other hand. It was a short screwdriver and it was dripping, dripping red...

Interruption female voice (FV): You're a drama king, mate. Tell 'em the truth.

Resume male narrator (MN): All right! All right! She was using the screwdriver to open a tin of baked beans.

Interruption FV: You enjoyed the beans, man!

Resume MN: The beans tasted good! They were hot! But, eight per cent battery! I need to continue, right?

Anyway, the beans didn't come until later. First I needed to sort out what I came here for. I managed to stand up. For a few minutes the hotel was spinning around me. I almost expected to look out of the window and see a giant's foot pushing down on some pedals. Then he must have eased on the brakes cos the place slowed down and stopped.

•

I made it up the stairs this time. That cat must have known it was a good idea to keep out of my way. Up one flight, then another, to the second floor.

It was pretty mash-up. Doors and walls smashed down and the wallpaper hanging off from the floods after the pipes got jacked out. And, oh yeah, the junior arsonists must have held a start-a-fire contest on opposite ends of the landing.

But I found my realignment room. Or more like it found me. Just walking towards it, I felt like my ears were going to burst, like it was pulling me in and shoving me away at the same time. I had to push my feet hard into the ruined carpet to make my brain take a proper look. The door was hanging on one hinge. Must have been one angry kid who managed that. Those doors were heavy. I should know – I spent nights hammering against one until my fists hurt so bad I couldn't open them.

I made myself go in. And ... the washbasin, the bed, the toilet, it was all gone. My old room was just a space between four walls and a ceiling that had gone all saggy from the water leaking above. I ran over to the corner where the bed used to be. The carpet came away in my hands. I'd taken the screwdriver from downstairs but I didn't need it. The floorboard was already loose. I levered it up, looking for the little roll of plastic.

My darling Ruby, this was why I came back. It was for you. Everything was, Ruby. All of it. I'm not making excuses for what happened but we did it for you.

I was driving the car. I've always admitted it. And anyway, they found me in the driver's seat. They probably had to prise my fingers off the wheel before they dumped me on the stretcher and took me away. And yeah, I was going too fast. And yeah, I wasn't even old enough to drive the car in the first place. But we didn't have any choice. Me and Tess had planned it down to the second. I'd pull up at the end of the road as soon as her dad had gone off to work. Tess had a friend in Liverpool who'd put us up for a while.

But Tess's sister gave us away. Her brother was parked round the bend. He pulled out in front of us. I spun the wheel too hard and hit the tree.

Tess.

I wrote a letter to her mum. I tried to say sorry. The prison never let me send it.

And you, Ruby. Tess had strapped you in, good and

proper. Maybe you jerked against the straps in your baby seat but you were all right.

So when they gave me that picture of you, I thought I'd never let it go. You're grinning at me and your teeth are just starting to come through. It was the first time I noticed you've got wriggly thin eyebrows like Tess, but my nose stuck underneath. Nan said that the gene carrying our nose is armour-plated. It hits every generation hard. Your arms are reaching out like you want to hug me. I can close my eyes and draw a map of every dimple and wrinkle in your knees. And when they brought me back in here after the realignment sessions, I'd wake up and find your picture in my hand.

They moved me out without any warning. I didn't have time to take you with me but now I'd come back.

I stuck my hand under the wood and stretched my fingers as far as I could. Nothing. I tried to look but I didn't need to. I knew the exact place. You weren't there.

And that was it. It felt like the wave was gonna come. I was just going to lie on the floor and let it clean me away.

Then I heard, "Got a problem?"

She—

Interruption FV: She? I ain't your cat's mother!

Resume MN: Damn, Ruby! This girl can do hard-face better than my nan!

So. Yeah. Maria was standing by the broke-down door.

She said, "I got your picture."

Then she just turned and walked off. I followed her, up more and more stairs until she pushed open the door and that's where we are now.

Maria calls it her room of love and dreams. I wasn't the only one who'd been hiding a picture. When the demolition crew moved out, Maria came back to find her picture. It was her older brother, Kyle. He'd joined the army, gone off to fight and was still missing. Then Maria got digging around the other rooms and found loads more photos. This is one of the driest rooms. She thought they'd be safe, in case anyone came looking. Mums, dads, brothers, sisters, babies, smiling, blowing kisses, caught shy and not ready. Our families are out there. And we'll never see them again.

Because that's what we signed up for. The water's gonna sweep away the buildings and we'll be the junk that lands up on other people's shores. One by one, dotted round the world in the places that no one else wants to go to. We'll be free. Yeah. As long as we change our names, change who we are. As long as we keep far, far away. As long as we never contact our families. Never contact each other. Never ever talk about what happened in these rooms. That's the deal. Some kids don't mind that. They've been scratching their own living almost since they were babies. But me, it's different. Nan's still out there. She was always fighting my corner. And then there's you, Ruby. How can I be free and you don't even know I'm alive?

The plane's disappeared and me and Maria have lit some candles. It sounds like there's fireworks in Churchill Square, but it must be the arsonists' oil bottles going off. We're gonna open some more tins. We've got beer, too. There's boxes of rice pudding and beans and booze in the cellars in the basement. Maria says the grub's stashed in the service tunnels next to the old therapy rooms. When I think about them, I start shaking again but Maria's arm is round me now.

Period of on/off time: Estimated 7 hours, 13 minutes, 42 seconds.

•

Day ZERO.

I don't need no plane to tell me that. We're all supposed to be out of here before sunset.

Three per cent battery. I don't know why I'm bothering anyway. They're gonna search us big time when we reach the gates. All the scanners. Whizzing up and down the bits even my nan never saw. If they find this on me, I'll be back in the van with the bars on it. Back in hardcore realignment. Back on the meds. They told us they could keep us there indefinite. You'd be older than I am now, Ruby, before I came out.

But now the sun's just coming up over the sea. The waves are creeping backwards and forwards like they're saving their energy; waiting for their big moment. I should find Emo and tell him that the Make Out Plan wasn't dead after all. Or tell him more than that. How having him on my side was the best thing for me. He was the one who saw me struggling, the morning after the first therapy. He picked up my spoon and made sure that soup got into my mouth, though he could hardly keep his own hand moving in a straight line. But I don't want to say goodbye to him because that seems too much like a final thing. I want to think of him as Emo, the man with a plan, full of mad ideas that somehow always fall right.

Soon the sirens are gonna go off. Then evacuation begins and the experiment ends. The public voted us out, but hey, they still get their spectacular finale.

Somewhere over the wall, in another town, Ruby, you're old enough to know you should have a dad. I don't reckon Tess's mum will tell you much about me. It's selfish but I want you to know I loved you. Maria said she used to go up to the wall and press her ears to the bricks. She was sure she could hear her brother crying on the other side.

She's still asleep. She said she used to have nightmares, too, but being here, surrounded by people full of love, made her calm. She's not joining the evacuation. She doesn't want to be somewhere strange. She doesn't want to be alone.

She doesn't have to be alone.

Less than one per cent battery now. I have a choice to make, Ruby. I can follow the sirens up to the main gate and take my place in the queue for the scan booths.

Or I can crouch down next to Maria and take her hand. I can wake her up and remind her. The sirens aren't blasting yet. We're in the room of love and dreams. Maybe there's hope, too.

Whatever happens, whichever way, I love you.

This is a transcript of an unverified audio recording kindly donated by Ms Ruby Stride, founder of the Clean Sweep Truth and Forgiveness Project. Easy-read and audible versions are available free for schools and politicians.

Suggested further reading:

Prison Highs: A Collection of Remastered Screengrabs of Overhead Views of Brightonstone Behaviour Realignment Camp
Private collection but research requests considered.

The Public Sway: Essays on the Cultural Impact of Reality TV and the Public Vote edited by Ruby Stride
Published by the Clean Sweep Truth and Forgiveness Project

Errol Maurice Ovenden v HM Prison Institute
(Annotated executive summary of civil case by plaintiff seeking compensation for false imprisonment, mental trauma and invasion of privacy.)
May only be accessed via Freedom of Information request process.

The Grand Hotel: An Architectural Oddity
(Including a detailed map of Victorian cellars, mid-20th century bunkers and reinforced service tunnels.)

Brightonstone Below: A 3-D reimagining of the city's subterranean tunnel networks.
The installation posits the theory that the network spread beyond Brightonstone and into the Downs. No evidence has been presented to prove or refute the claim.

IRIDESCENT ADOLESCENT

•

Phoebe Roy

When the first feather came, two months after her thirteenth birthday, Nathalie plucked it out and laid it in the treasure box she kept on the big dresser in her bedroom. The box was made of silky dark wood and, apart from the feather, it contained four things. She had a little velvet bag with her baby teeth inside, that she had kept because she used to think she might be able to do a spell with them, and she had one photograph from her parents' wedding, that had 'Mazel Tov, Carmel and Arnab' written across the bottom in pink cursive letters. She also had the note Josh Franklin had written wishing her a happy birthday and finally she had the necklace, a gift from her great-aunt, Auntie Apphia in America. The feather was only about five centimetres long and in dim light its vanes looked brown, but when the sun bounced off it, it shone bronze.

The necklace from her great aunt wasn't really the sort of thing she'd buy for herself – it was gold and filigreed with a gem at the centre. If you looked closely, you could see that what appeared to be a pattern of twisted twigs clawed around the gem was actually a tangle of clasped skeletal hands and wings. It made her feel peculiar when she looked at it, and the stone winked and warmed in her hand as she cupped it there. When Carmel saw it, she had raised her eyebrows and opened her mouth as if she were about to speak, but then shook her head and said nothing.

The feather lay next to the note from Josh Franklin, sparkling slightly as if it knew something. At first the tiny dent it had left just below her collarbone had bled, but it soon healed.

•

After the first feathers appeared, Nathalie began to wake early and ravenous, and would creep downstairs to get something to eat. Once her mother caught her, cramming entire sheets of smoked salmon into her mouth while clutching a box of ladoos under one arm.

She caught the air-bathed smell of her skin whenever she moved, freshly mineral and greenly salty, as if she'd been out all night running through the trees. Her curls streamed down her back and there were new feathers every day. Now she only plucked out the ones that could be seen. When she got out of the bath she turned to face away from the mirror and twisted to see the line of bronze marching down her spine. They lay flat and almost invisible during the day, apart from when something angered her, at which she could feel the feathers standing up. At night, though, they unfurled and rippled when she sat cross-legged and solemn in front of her bedroom mirror. She thought about the sea all the time, and took the note from Josh out of her treasure box and slept with it rolled up tightly and clutched in her palm.

•

The hunger was new, because Nathalie used to have to be coaxed to eat. When she was seven her parents had become so worried by it that they spent long hours trying to come up with a way to persuade her to try different food. Carmel shared her concern with her mother, who suggested that they start sending Nathalie to shul on festivals, where there would be lots of different foods for her to try, away from the watchful and anxious eyes of her parents.

"It's time she started taking an interest in her heritage anyway," said Arnab.

Carmel then suggested that it would be nice for Nathalie to go to the temple with her cousins on her father's side. She was given delicious things – spiced potatoes and pastries, balls of dough covered in sugar, miniature squares of matzo with a smear of cream cheese and little flutes of salmon – and she would light candles and sing songs with her cousins and aunties and uncles. She thought about how lucky she was to be such a pretty shade of gold; belonging with all of them but different enough that she seemed her own invention. Still she barely ate. She felt oppressed by how solid her bones seemed and kept a collection of fairy pictures, which she looked at every evening under her duvet with a torch. She longed for hollowness.

The same year, her mother asked her how she would like to go and stay with her Auntie Apphia in California for the summer. She knew Apphia was an artist and lived in a house on stilts at the edge of a forest of coastal redwoods. She knew the stream that flowed outside was clean enough to drink from, and that you could see deer and mountain lions out of the wrap-around glass windows. She nodded her head eagerly and looked forward to her adventure. Her father took her shopping to buy her her own special suitcase and a pink leather wallet to put her passport in.

She brandished both these items proudly at the flight attendant, who seated her next to a friendly woman. She thought she would be afraid of the plane but she soon found her strongest feeling was boredom, so she got out of her seat and began to lope up and down the aisles, sending moody looks in either direction. She felt someone gently touch her arm and she looked down at the hand first, then up at its owner. It was a kind-looking man who asked where her mother and father were. She raised her eyes to his and his smile died. He gulped and looked away; she felt a strange heat behind her eyeballs, as if they were burning. She continued her prowling.

•

At first, staying at Auntie Apphia's felt strange – there were no set mealtimes or bedtimes, not like at home. Her great-aunt seemed to have countless friends and colleagues who appeared some time in the morning and stayed late into the night. They talked about politics and art and history, but they also talked about what they'd been watching on TV and had friendly rows about which of them would be the most use after an apocalypse. Some of these people were over eighty years old, which to Nathalie may as well have been a thousand; they had all survived apocalypses. They came and went in shifts and their voices filled the house. They pinched Nathalie's cheeks and called her a shaina maideleh; one man asked loudly if this was the schvartze's child. There was a silence, then Apphia ordered him out, explaining afterwards that he had not been invited.

The sea lived in the house's corners and in Apphia's paintings. The canvas she was working on covered the whole of one wall in the studio and showed a cliff in cross-section, so detailed that it made Nathalie's eyes hurt to look at it too closely. In the morning, when her great-aunt came to wake her, she would bring with her a thick salt air, and Nathalie could see damp prints on the stairs. They weren't shaped like human feet but Nathalie couldn't tell exactly what they were.

When she left, her great-aunt hugged her tightly, dropped one kiss on her forehead and gave her a tiny turquoise egg flecked with little gold splashes. Nathalie asked if her aunt had painted it because she had never seen such depth and purity of colour in nature. Apphia hesitated before saying that she had.

•

Years after the summer in California, Arnab suggested it would be nice to go on a trip to the seaside for Nathalie's twelfth birthday, which was in March and that year fell on a Saturday. They decided on Brighton because it was the closest to home and because there were cousins they could visit on the way back. As soon as they came within sight of the coast, Nathalie felt like jumping out of the car and tearing down to the beach. She kept herself still by wrapping both arms round her ribcage and tried not to picture herself running into the waves, the foam hissing round her ankles. Carmel didn't say much that day but she kept glancing at the water, leaving Arnab to keep up the conversation.

"Do you fancy a dip, beti?" he asked when they were installed in a café full of wrought-iron furniture painted white and with a single rose in a slim glass vase on each table. Nathalie looked up with an eager expression, but then caught the twinkle in his eye and realized he had been teasing. But her mother spoke up.

"I'd like a dip, jaan," she said.

Nathalie's father laughed and said that both his girls were tougher than him. Then he bet Carmel that she wouldn't have the nerve, calling her bubbeleh, as he always did. Carmel shook her husband's hand and laughed, because she was like her own father and never turned down a bet. Arnab and Nathalie joined in the laughter, but then Nathalie saw an air of expectancy settle over her mother. As soon as the bill came, she leaped to her feet.

"Come on, beti-leh," she said. Taking Nathalie's hand, she began to hurry down to the beach.

They tore off their shoes and socks and ran towards the water, squealing when the chill pebbles touched their toes. Arnab got out his camera and took shot after shot of Nathalie and Carmel, hand in hand and ankle-deep in the surf, the waves clinging to their skin like little white lace-frilled socks. In profile, Carmel looked fierce; it was only when she faced you that she appeared softer and prettier. Nathalie had inherited her mother's sharp jawline and Arnab's Roman nose, but her dark red curls were a mystery to them both. A breeze whipped up their hair, and anyone watching closely would have seen the neat necklace of little red dots on the nape of her mother's neck, and the tiny turquoise point piercing through the skin under her right ear, just for a moment, before she lifted a hand and smoothed her hair back down.

•

Six months after Nathalie's thirteenth birthday, a phone rang in a glass house on stilts at the foot of a forest in California, interrupting Apphia's morning painting. Normally she would leave it to ring, because she liked to make the most of the dawn light, but whoever it was kept hanging up and redialling. In the end, she balanced her brush on the edge of a jar of murky green water and went to answer it.

"You said it wouldn't happen to her," said Carmel, not bothering with a greeting. "You knew! You knew it would, when you promised it wouldn't."

"No," said Apphia, carefully. "I didn't promise, I said we had no way of knowing until she was older."

"Then why did you send her the necklace?" Carmel asked.

Apphia could picture Carmel breathing out of her nostrils as she always did when annoyed, like a bull.

"It's just a necklace," said Apphia gently.

Carmel was silent for a moment or two, then said, "Her feathers are a different colour to ours."

"Are they? What colour?"

"They're a sort of … bronze."

Apphia was silent for a moment. Then she said, "How fascinating. Did you know, for Homer blue and bronze were interchangeable? *The Iliad* is full of references to the bronze sky, so I wonder if—"

"If I destroyed the necklace, do you think it would reverse the process?"

"Oh darling, now why would you want to do a thing like that? She is part of a wonderful tradition, she has sisters all over the world…"

Carmel swallowed the lump that had appeared in her throat. "I don't want her to be different," she admitted.

"Caramel," said her aunt gently, using her childhood nickname, "she's already different."

•

From time to time, Nathalie would take the necklace out of her treasure box and put it on. The gem changed colour in different lights and Nathalie was surprised to find that of the few people she trusted enough to show it to, her mother saw it as blue, she saw it as bronze, and her best friend Chloe and her father both thought it was entirely clear, like a piece of quartz. Her great-aunt sent her a parcel, as she often did, and when Nathalie opened it, a peacock feather and a pastel sketch of a peacock fell out.

"My darling Natty," it read. "Please find enclosed some little curiosities for your treasure box. I know some people think peacock feathers are unlucky but they're so beautiful that I'm prepared to risk it. I do hope you feel the same. They're fascinating creatures, peacocks, and the quality of their feathers even more so. Their pigment is brown, but the structural arrangement of the feather's vanes (those are the pointy bits) make them appear that iridescent colour. Isn't that wonderful? The way they look is down to what they essentially and objectively *are* – nothing so pedestrian as pigmentation. Just a little tidbit for you, darling. Kisses to Mum and Dad, as always."

Nathalie folded up the letter and ran her thumb and forefinger over its folds until they were sharp enough to cut her. She set it down, then held up the peacock feather to one she had pulled from just under her ear – a tiny one, no larger than the joint of her little finger. Turning them over side by side, she could see no link between them. She shrugged and put them both in the box.

•

One night, Carmel and Arnab were lying in bed. Arnab was lying flat on his back with his hands clasped behind his neck. His head was turned slightly to the right, as if he was staring at the vase of dwarf roses on the bedside table.

"We should stop locking the doors at night," he said.

Carmel marked her place with her finger and looked over at him.

"For Nathalie," he continued. "If she's going to start needing to go out every evening."

"How did you know?" asked Carmel after a pause.

Arnab shrugged, almost imperceptibly. "She's started to smell just like you," he said. "And she's always hungry. I worry about her trying to come in through the window."

"We could give her a key," said Carmel, still watching him.

"That's a good idea. She could wear it on the necklace, if she started wearing it more," he said.

He reached up and kissed Carmel on the cheek, then he crescent-mooned himself up on his left side and closed his eyes. Almost instantly, he fell asleep.

•

A thousand years ago, four winged figures stood on the edge of a cliff at sunrise. The cliff overlooked a valley, holding two vast lakes, one on the eastern boundary and one on the west. The cliff was banded with rock running in pale red and rose veins, and the

191

rising sun turned the bands to flame. The figures were still, but their wings were outstretched and poised, like drawn swords, and each stood over six feet tall. If you were up on the clifftop with them, you would also have seen a fifth much smaller being, a human child sitting nearby with her knees drawn up. Calm rolled off the child and she showed no fear even as the creatures turned to her, each holding out a jewelled cup. She took each cup and drank deeply, then she wiped her mouth with the back of her hand.

•

Carmel and Arnab announced they would all be going to see Auntie Apphia over the Easter holidays to celebrate Nathalie's fifteenth birthday. Nathalie was furious at how much fun she'd miss, and her outrage only increased when her parents replied that nothing so important could possibly happen in just a week. Nathalie locked herself in her room but finally emerged, pouting, some time later. She grudgingly admitted she was looking forward to seeing her great-aunt again.

•

Apphia greeted them warmly, with a strange sparkle at the corner of each eye, and immediately set about installing them in the house, which was just as Nathalie remembered it. The endless visitors still came, some bringing with them boys of about her age. As soon as she saw them, she feigned lack of interest and sat herself in their midst reading magazines.

On the last night of their holiday, Arnab woke suddenly to a faintly metallic smell and a sound like faraway chimes. Even though the curtains were closed, the room was full of flat silver light, ironing the perspective from the furniture, and Carmel was nowhere to be seen. Drawing the curtains, he saw a full moon hanging watchfully in the sky as if it expected to be caught in a long-handled net, its craters standing in relief, giving it the look of a great glowing marble. The chimes grew louder and he stumbled out of the house, jamming on his shoes as he did so. He could feel his heart high up in his chest as he reached the beach. The sea was molten mercury in the moonlight, the waves crashing down like fistfuls of coins, rudely loud amid the silent night air. Arnab dropped down on to sand as white as sunbleached bones and sat watching the water while he waited.

He didn't have to wait long before one of the waves, turned by the dark into a slab of black jelly, was pierced by a creature bursting through its surface, a feathered turquoise blade with its wings folded behind it. It dived back under the next wave and disappeared. Next came another, also turquoise, which also dived back under the water, and then a third, bronze, which rose high into the sky and spread its wings, silhouetted against the moon. It threw back its head and made three harsh cries. Goose pimples shot through him as the figure beat its wings, once, twice, then folded them behind its shoulders and shot back down into the water, which closed over it like a medal dropped in ink. Even the waves seemed to quiet then, their scalloped edges nudging gently at the sand. Arnab smiled.

DEAR ASHA

·

Mary Bello

The atmosphere of her mother's birthplace smacked Asha in the face as soon as she stepped off the plane. The air, humid and heady, left an instant film of sweat on her tired limbs. She'd finally made it to Nigeria, although not in the circumstances she'd always imagined. In her fantasies Asha had come here with her mum, Bisi. Bisi had always promised they would visit when Asha graduated from university. They'd explore Lagos and Abuja before heading to Ondo City, where Bisi was born. Asha would get to know her grandparents and all the aunties, uncles and cousins that she'd heard thousands of stories about but never met. They'd stay up until the early hours, sitting by the light of oil lamps on the veranda at her grandparents' house, listening to family anecdotes and Ondo folklore while swatting away mosquitoes.

She'd eat soft, sweet agege bread for breakfast, hike up the Idanre Mountains and buy material to be sewn into dresses by local seamstresses. Her hair would be braided into a mass of tiny braids, so long you could sit on them. Kids in the village selling pure water on the roadside would follow her round, cheekily asking for a few naira, calling out 'oyinbo' and giggling at her freckles and green eyes. Instead she was here to bury her mother.

Eight months ago Asha sat with Bisi in a doctor's office, holding her hand and hoping for the best. On the way to the hospital, Asha looked for signs that all was well. But everything from the grey skies to the train delays seemed to scream bad news.

"Mrs Maxwell, I'm so sorry but the biopsy showed you have pancreatic cancer."

Asha stopped listening as soon as the heartbreaking sentence fell from the doctor's lips. The sound of him speaking was replaced by the intense pounding of her heart.

Then four more words pierced her consciousness. "Nine months at best." Nine months? Surely the doctor was wrong?

Bisi had thanked the consultant and left with a handful of leaflets and an appointment to see an oncologist.

"Mama, soon as we get home I'm going to do some research and see if there's some sort of treatment programme we can get you on. If we can't afford it, you can use my uni fund or we can start a fundraising page. The doctor could even be wrong. There was a report on the news the other day about people living for *years* with cancer. Chronic cancer management, I think they called it..." Asha could hear that her voice was panicked and high-pitched but she couldn't control herself.

Bisi sighed and said, "Darling, we saw the scans last month and the biopsy has just confirmed things. I haven't felt right for a long time. Let's just stay positive and pray. I promise you I will fight this but let's be realistic, OK?"

She suddenly looked older than her forty-seven years. She drew Asha into a hug and the two of them stood together in the hospital corridor.

From the moment of the diagnosis, Asha read book after book; she contacted clinics in Finland and

Canada and put her mother on special curative diets. There was Reiki, Ayurvedic methods, oil pulling, meditation and evangelical churches promising miraculous healing, all squeezed in between visits from the Macmillan nurse and trips to the hospital. Every night Asha would plead with God for a cure.

Seven months was all it took. Asha was with her mother at the end. She had left her sixth-form college a week after the consultation and studied from their terraced house in Catford, only attending to sit her final exams. She cared for Bisi, bathing her, making dinner and sleeping in her room. It was just the two of them – Asha's father, James, had left ten years ago and they'd barely heard from him in the last five. Together they watched Nollywoood movies and episodes of *Desmond's* and *Friends*. Asha learned about her mother's first love and the time she spent in Paris on a student exchange programme. In the French capital she rode mopeds, sneaked backstage at a gig, kissed the lead singer of a band and tried her hand at modelling. ("Yes, Mama! You knew how to turn up!" Asha had snapped her fingers and laughed, enjoying the fact that her mother had once been wild and reckless.)

•

Asha passed in a dreamlike state through passport control to baggage claim to arrivals and stood staring at the sea of faces in Murtala Muhammed airport. Would she recognize her auntie Loladé? She had only ever seen her in pictures and most of them were from the 80s and 90s, when Loladé had still been a kid. There was a thirteen-year age gap between Loladé and Bisi. Her mother hadn't spoken about her sister much but, when she did, it was with a detached fondness, as though she was an old friend – fun, irresponsible, distant.

Asha headed towards the exit and stood against a wall to the side of the revolving doors. Her baggage was arranged at her feet except for the old battered red-leather suitcase her mother had told her to take, with instructions to open it after the funeral. She held the small case tightly in front of her. The key that would unlock it was tucked into her handbag. The case had lived on top of her mother's wardrobe, padlocked. When she was little she would climb on to her mum's squidgy divan, pull it down and play at pretending her teddy was Paddington Bear.

She could feel her hair shrinking and getting puffy in the humid air, so she pulled it into a high bun. The clock on the arrivals board read 10 a.m. and her flight had landed at 9.20. Why wasn't her auntie here already? Anxious, Asha sighed and started to bite her bottom lip.

"Madam, do you need taxi? Shall I carry your bags?" A man in a cream shirt and brown trousers approached her.

"Oya, move on, jarre!" A woman with dark-brown skin and a red-tinted low fade appeared and ushered the man away. She was wearing a yellow maxi dress and brown leather sandals. She turned to Asha with a broad grin and exclaimed, "Shy-Shy Baby! Ah, ah, finally we meet."

Her auntie drew Asha into a tight embrace, swamping her with the scent of Chanel No. 5. When they parted, Loladé had tears in her eyes and she gripped Asha's face in her palms. Shy-Shy Baby was the nickname her mum had started using when she'd been a clingy toddler. The nickname had stuck and Bisi had always used it. But now, hearing the name from someone else just seemed a little wrong. Asha felt embarrassed by the outpouring of affection and the constant eye contact.

•

It was an hour's drive from the airport to her auntie's house in Lekki, a smart air-conditioned duplex near the beach, away from the heavy hustle and bustle of Lagos city centre. Loladé had talked as fast as she drove her red Mercedes G-Class, filling Asha in on her life. She worked as a stylist and had a boyfriend who was a musician. Her world seemed a far cry from her sister's, working as an accountant in England on a modest salary. Asha felt carsick and miserable, half-listening to Loladé's tales while she took in the country.

She saw women with babies strapped to their backs, carrying raffia bowls on their heads filled with tomatoes and peppers. There were people squashed on to the seats of okadas and one stopped beside them momentarily in traffic, the passengers a father and his three little girls who wore bright pink hijabs. She breathed in the acrid smell of petrol and palm trees that clung to the air. The atmosphere bewitched her despite the heaviness of her heart.

Bisi had proudly told Asha about Ondo and Nigeria when she was a kid. There were tales about the city where Bisi had grown up, the energy of Lagos, the traditions of their people and orishas – the Yoruba gods and goddesses, lessons on their native dialect and scary stories about the Biafran war in the late 60s. But nothing compared to actually seeing it.

"And this is your home from home!" Auntie Loladé cried, swinging open the ornate wooden front door. "The house girl will show you to your room. BLESSING? BLESSING! WHERE ARE YOU?"

A skinny girl a few years younger than Asha appeared. She had three long vertical tribal markings on each cheek and jaw-length braids.

"Sorry, ma, I was jus' hangin' out di washing." She genuflected in front of Loladé and then turned to do the same to Asha, bowing deeply. "Welcome, madam, I hope you will enjoy your time in Nigeria." Then Blessing ran outside and grabbed Asha's bags from the car.

"Your room is on the second floor, third door on the left," Loladé told her. 'You've got your own bathroom. Go and settle in. We'll have lunch in half an hour."

Blessing led her up the stairs, proudly showing Asha a beautiful room, triple the size of her box room in London and decorated in a minimalist style. When Blessing left, Asha flopped down on the bed. She watched a gecko as it defied the laws of gravity and lazily progressed across the ceiling. Blessing had told her they'd have pounded yam and ogbono soup for lunch. "I prepared it myself," she'd said with a broad grin, revealing very white teeth.

Asha felt guilty about that. She felt guilty about Blessing, full stop. Only fourteen, she worked for and lived with Loladé, who in turn paid her school fees and sent Blessing's parents a monthly stipend. A situation so alien to Asha but, "a necessary transaction when you live in a country with no social welfare," Loladé would tell her later on that evening.

Asha drifted off and dreamed of flying in a helicopter at night, leaving behind her mother, who had not managed to get in before takeoff. When she woke up, she had wet cheeks. Even sleep didn't stop tears from falling.

•

Lunch was two hours late due to Asha's unscheduled nap. Eventually Loladé had knocked hard on her bedroom door. "Ah! You no wan chop? Oya, come down and eat, o."

It was delicious. They ate with their hands from blue bowls. Asha loved rolling the pounded yam into smooth bite-sized balls in one hand before dipping them into the slick ogbono, watching strands of the soup draw out and slip off before hungrily swallowing. This was the first proper meal she'd had in the six weeks since her mother's passing. She'd already lost a stone and her wardrobe was full of clothes that hung off her angular, jutting collarbones. Melody, Asha's best friend, had taken to sitting with her at mealtimes, back in London, trying to get her to eat. But Asha would only pick at whatever was on the plate.

After eating they went into the spacious living room, Loladé clutching a bottle of wine and two glasses. Nneka's 'My Love, My Love' was playing from speakers embedded in the ceiling. Asha hadn't listened to the song for a while. She'd danced to it last Valentine's with Bisi after her boyfriend Danny had broken up with her. Both mother and daughter had declared February 14th Anti-Valentine's Day that year. They ate distinctly non-romantic food (fajitas) and watched *Thelma and Louise*. When Asha confessed 'My Love, My Love' had been her and Danny's song, Bisi had jumped on to the armchair and said, "Let's reclaim it! Let's make it ours." The two of them had danced and sung at the top of their voices.

Everything was slick and stylish in Loladé's world – so different to Asha's colourful home back in England, which was all red chinoiserie rugs and purple bedroom walls. Thinking of their house made the threat of tears sting again. Bisi had told Asha that the house would be hers and the mortgage was paid off. But how could she live in the home that had once been so full of her mother's spirit and was now so silent?

The two women curled up at either end of the long white sofa. Despite being less than two weeks away from eighteen, Asha had declined the wine.

"Look at you, such a good girl. Like Mama!" Loladé held up her hands in mock surrender. "OK, OK, no wine for Asha. So, Bisi's girl, how are you? Really?"

But before Asha could answer, the lights went off

and the sound of the AC cut out.

"Ah! Nepa, don' take light again, o! Don't worry, we'll resume normal service in a second." Loladé's voice constantly flipped between fast, Yoruba-accented pidgin English and a slightly American/English vibe. As promised, the lights and air conditioning suddenly kicked in again. "Thank God for generators, eh? So, tell me, how are you doing?"

How was she doing? Devastated, broken, confused, angry, sad, hollow.

Asha shrugged, "OK, I guess."

"Oh darling, come on. I know we haven't met before but we're family. You can talk to me."

Silence.

"OK, if you're not going to talk, I'll talk. I only have you to myself for two nights. Before everyone else descends like you're Ondo's answer to Beyoncé!"

Asha giggled at that. Loladé began to tell Asha about her mother's childhood and although some of the stories Asha knew, some she didn't. Loladé explained about the Yoruba funeral customs and Asha took comfort from the belief that death was not the end but rather the progression of life to another plane.

The connection she had with her mother would remain strong whether she could see her in this world or not. There would be street processions and all-night parties with food and dancing to celebrate the life Bisi had led. And yes, there would be tears because she wasn't physically there – but her spirit was. They must hold on to that.

As she relaxed in her auntie's company, Asha began to ask questions. Why did Mum never come back to Nigeria? Why didn't Loladé ever visit?

"To tell you the truth, I don't have a good excuse. It's easy to kid yourself that letters and phone calls are enough. I would constantly say to myself, I'll go next year. But next year never came. When Bisi moved to the UK, I felt like she left us all behind. Such a foolish thing to hold on to and now she's gone I…" She stopped for a moment. "Anyway, as for your mum coming here, after the way things had been during the military rule in the 80s, she decided a life in the west was for her. But it's changed so much here…"

"Do you know much about my dad?" Asha asked. "I feel so guilty about him not knowing Mum has died. I feel like it's my fault he won't be at the funeral."

"Kini?! That useless man! Would he have come even if he'd known?" Angered and slightly tipsy, Loladé had switched to her more Yoruba accent. "That cheating waste of space! Ode buruku!"

Asha cocked her head to one side. "Hold on. Did you say cheating? Did Dad cheat on my mum?" The thought made Asha feel sick.

Loladé had straightened up a little with the sobering thought of remembering who she was speaking to. "Look, don't listen to me. I'm just running my mouth. Your mum must have told you I speak before I think?"

Asha nodded slowly, trying to squash down thoughts of her father being unfaithful, she wasn't ready to explore that on top of everything. Not yet anyway.

"Bisi, babe! She was the best of us, you know? She's the one your grandparents are proud of. The rest of us always paled in comparison. Perfect grades, perfect career, perfect life in London." Loladé smiled, wrinkled her nose and stuck out her tongue when she ended her sentence, a mannerism Asha shared when she was excited about something.

For the first time Asha noticed how alike they looked. Despite Asha being more of a caramel colour with long gangly limbs, in comparison to her aunt's smooth dark complexion and diminutive, curvy body, they had the same Nubian nose, prominent cheekbones and wide spacing between almond-shaped eyes. They were very much family.

As the day slipped away and turned to night, Asha found herself feeling grateful for the bond growing between them.

•

That first night in Lagos, like every night since her mum died, sleep was fitful. Again she dreamed of Bisi. This time her mother was sat at the kitchen table back in Catford, its blue and white gingham cloth covered in spots of blood. Asha was in the back garden watching through the window as her mother tried to wipe the spots away. Her dad entered the room and asked her mum if she needed any help; she shook her head. "I'm sorry, darling," her mum mouthed to Asha before lifting a hand to cover her lips and coughing up blood until it began to spill out of her palm and on to the floor. Asha banged on the window and started screaming. She screamed so loud that Loladé rushed into the room and shook her awake.

"Shh, it's OK, Asha. You're OK. It was just a dream." Loladé sat on the bed and held Asha tight until her screams turned into racking sobs then gentle crying. After what seemed like an age, she fell into a dreamless, exhausted sleep.

•

Loladé took Asha to Balogun market the next morning. Kunle, her odd-job man and sometimes driver, drove them in her SUV to the sound of Fela Kuti's *The Best of the Black President*. Loladé sang along, danced in her seat and mimed the trumpet sections while Asha peered out of the window, taking in more of Lagos.

When they arrived, the market's chaos unfolded before her like a blossoming flower. Asha quickly got separated from Loladé and found herself lost in the colours of fabric piled on small stalls and high on the smell of meat being barbecued by food sellers. She bought some beautiful blue and pink coral beads for far more than they were worth because she hadn't gotten to grips with haggling, and found striking paintings of women carrying children in vibrant hues and bought two.

Asha was drawn to a shop playing old-school Afrobeats that her mum used to listen to. The interior was wall-to-wall CDs. The owner, a friendly man who insisted he was her long-lost uncle after finding out her mother's maiden name, pressed a free CD into her hand. Asha bought another ten despite the fact she didn't own a CD player. Then she remembered her aunt and pulled out her phone from her handbag. Loladé had called her about twenty times. She texted to let her know where she was.

They met outside the shop and continued walking through the crowded streets. Men called out to them as they passed by.

"You no see dis babe? She dey bust my skeroo well well!" one man cried.

While Asha blushed, Loladé retorted in pidgin and kissed her teeth before sashaying off.

Asha complained that the heat was making her hair unmanageable. She'd tried to pull it back into a topknot but couldn't get her edges to lay. Random sections of hair sprung loose and curled in different ways.

"It does look kinda wild," said Loladé. "Don't worry, my lady will fix you up."

Off they went through a maze of streets until they stopped by a very narrow shop where a rotund woman wearing a pink T-shirt and a green wrapper and headscarf leaned in the doorway.

Soon enough, Asha's head was being yanked this way and that like she was a child, fingers moving at lightning speed. When Asha winced at the tightness of some braids, Loladé shouted with mock horror at the hairdresser, "Please o, no dey make my pikin suffer!" That soon became their catchphrase and for the first time since her mother's death, Asha felt her soul get a little lighter.

By the time Asha's last waist-length box braid was put in place, her butt was sore from the four hours spent sitting down and her legs ached from all the walking they'd done. She stretched gratefully as soon as she was released from the stylist's chair, admiring her new hair in the mirror. She liked how different the braids made her look and feel – a little more grown-up, a little more confident.

Outside of the salon, though only 6 p.m., the cloud-scattered sky had begun to take on a hazy deep orange and cool blue hue. Asha's stomach growled fiercely.

"Let's call Kunle and head back towards Lekki. We could get something to eat by one of the beaches," said Loladé.

•

The car pulled up to the barrier at the entrance to Eleko beach, Loladé paid the 500 naira fee and they continued through to the car park where *area boys* – the local street hustlers – were waiting to help them 'park and protect their cars'. Loladé handed over another 500. Asha and Loladé hopped out of the car and immediately the boys started directing Kunle into a parking slot.

Asha slipped off her black sliders as soon as they'd connected with the beach so she could feel the tiny grains of sand underfoot. They walked alongside the makeshift bars and restaurants that lined the beachfront. Eleko was an endless plain of golden sand. Impossibly tall palm trees lined the beach, their skinny trunks ending in a sudden spray of deep green shiny leaves that swayed softly in the breeze.

"This is my favourite beach. You don't get too many tourists here and at night, hey, the way it comes to *life!*" Loladé said, doing a little body roll to an imaginary beat on the word *life* before she steered Asha towards her favourite suya seller.

He was about Asha's age, dressed in a faded Arsenal football shirt, navy shorts and flip-flops. Flames licked at the skewered meat that stood over the open wood fire. He wiped sweat from his brow with the back of his hand, finished wrapping up an order for the people in front of them and gave them a lopsided grin. "Kilonshele! What would you ladies like?"

Asha smiled and said, "Two, please. I'll get this," She thrust a hand into her bag and pulled out a wad of rolled-up naira notes.

They headed down towards the foreshore with their food and found a spot to sit and eat. A small group of white men in their twenties lounged on a huge cream blanket under a green parasol. They spoke Dutch, sipped on beers from a cool box and skinned up gbana from the tiny plastic bags hawkers sold on the sly.

Asha and Loladé sat side by side on the warm sand, legs hunched. Asha's braids danced in the wind and they ate the hot, spicy street food while watching the sea. She tried to imagine her parents here – happy and carefree, young and in love. They'd met in Nigeria when her father had been working on secondment as an English teacher at the school where Bisi had her first job as an admissions officer. She knew from her mother that the two of them had visited Lekki most weekends when they first got together. She still didn't understand why her parents had split so unexpectedly and now Loladé had left her with more unanswered questions.

"Something on your mind?" Loladé said as she sucked meat juices off the tips of her fingers.

"What happened with my parents?" Asha threw out, and this time she was determined not to let the conversation slide without an answer.

Loladé's brow furrowed ever so slightly but she said nothing, looking out towards the Gulf of Guinea.

Asha turned to her. "I feel so unsteady about everything, you know? Mum's gone. Dad's not in my life. I never knew why they split. It was as though, because I was a kid, I didn't deserve any answers. Mum was so angry and it felt like my father just let us slip away from him. Please just tell me the truth. Was there someone else?"

Loladé faced Asha. "Yes."

Years ago, when they'd been a happy family, her parents had fit perfectly. They were the kind of couple who laughed a lot, who could look at the other and know what was being said without a single word. They looked right together. Both tall and slim, Bisi possessed a neat black bob, medium-brown skin and an oval face, with a slightly square set jaw, high cheekbones and slanted wide eyes. Her father, James – who was fifteen years older – had a handsome, distinguished look about him with striking pale green eyes framed by laughter lines and thick-lensed reading glasses. His mousy brown hair, shot through with grey, seemed to have a mind of its own, growing this way and that. He always smelled of coffee and tobacco, a smell she'd found comforting. He was funny, charming and slightly oddball, borderline obsessed with comic-book superheroes. James was the head of English at a local secondary school, while Bisi worked part-time in a bank, studying in the evenings.

Life had been great until Asha was seven. She

remembered how they would always spend Sundays together. Her dad would wake her up around 8 a.m. and she'd follow him down the stairs, clutching her careworn stuffed bunny, Sable, and together they'd make breakfast while her mother had a lie-in. Asha would use her blue plastic cutter to turn toast into heart shapes before spreading them with butter and strawberry jam while her dad made coffee and scrambled eggs. Then they'd go into her parents' bedroom and pile on to the bed. She'd watch cartoons lying on her stomach on top of the duvet in between them. Afterwards, if the weather was good, they'd be off on adventures in their rusty old Ford Focus. They'd visit Leeds Castle or drive down to Brighton and eat sandwiches on the pier. If the weather was bad, a Lovers Rock album would be slipped on to her dad's record player and her parents would dance around the living room. Her mum swayed soulfully while her dad moved in an awkward but enthusiastic fashion. Before long one of them would pull Asha off the sofa and into the mix.

Then one Sunday they had an almighty row. It started in the morning and after an hour of shouting and no breakfast in bed, Asha's mum came into her room, red-eyed.

"Asha, can you brush your teeth and get dressed? I'm taking you to Sammy's."

Normally Asha loved going to her friend Sammy's but her parents had promised they'd go for a picnic on that day.

"I don't want to," she'd said.

Bisi's hair was still wrapped up in a black scarf and she was wearing the shapeless orange dress she normally only wore around the house. "Asha, do not test me today. Get ready. We are going to Sammy's. Now!"

As Bisi marched Asha out of the door, she turned to see her father pulling a suitcase from the cupboard under the stairs. When she came home that evening, he was gone.

Initially she stayed over at her dad's tiny one-bedroom flat in Highbury every other weekend but over time the visits began to feel awkward, conversations forced. When her dad took a teaching job in Scotland, sporadic phone calls, emails and birthday cards dwindled to nothing.

"The only reason your mum wouldn't have said

anything was to protect you. You were too young when it all happened. She wanted to tough it out and distance herself from him. She didn't want to stop James from seeing you but he found being around your mum too hard. He still loved her. But he'd been incredibly stupid and there was no going back. He found it easier to completely shut himself off, I guess."

How could her father do that to them? "Mum was devastated when he left. How did she find out?"

"Your dad tried to end the affair and the woman got in touch with your mum and told her everything."

Asha was confused, angry and felt more questions bubbling up to the surface. She needed to understand why he didn't fight harder for her mum or at least fight to try and see her when they got divorced.

"Maybe you should get in touch with him when you get back to London. What I said last night was a little harsh. Sometimes people just do stupid things."

"Don't they just," Asha muttered, almost to herself.

"Tell him about your mum. He'd want to know. He'd want to be there for you."

"Yeah, maybe," replied Asha and she turned to face the sea again.

•

The following morning they were loading Loladé's Mercedes with bags ready to head to Ondo. Kunle dutifully held open the back door so they could both get in. Just before he started the engine, Asha remembered the old red suitcase. Loladé hollered and Blessing swiftly brought it out, setting it on the passenger seat as they finally embarked on the four-hour drive to Ondo, 90s R&B blaring from the stereo.

Asha slept for the first hour, waking to find her head in Loladé's lap. She sat up and rubbed her eyes. "Sorry," she said, sheepishly pulling a face.

"So you should be, you snore like an old man!"

Asha opened her mouth to make a smart retort but before the words came out the car pulled to an abrupt stop. Four policemen armed with large guns walked towards the front of the car. One of the policemen sauntered to the driver's window and motioned for Kunle to wind it down.

"Oga, wetin dey trouble you? Make us jus' pass now. We need to get to a funeral," Loladé exclaimed loudly.

"Madam, we all have places to be. You think I wan'

waka for dis road all day? I do it for you and your small girl. Chief." He turned his attention to Kunle. "What do you have for me?"

"Brudda, I no get anyting. Nah only old kobo in my pocket."

"Ey? Who are you calling brudda? Make you give me somethin' before your head rolls on this floor today!"

Loladé kissed her teeth and cursed under her breath before handing Kunle some rolled-up notes, which were passed on to the officer.

He snatched the money and counted it slowly. "Hmm, is that all? Small, small naira. Anyway, because you are carrying fine-fine cargo, I'll let you go."

They drove away slowly.

"What was all that about?" Asha asked.

"Roadblocks, checkpoints," Loladé said matter-of-factly. "The police and army set them up, stop you and ask for money before you continue your journey. Apparently it's to keep road users safe from crime. If you ask me, the only criminals are them – extortion under the guise of protection."

"Surely it's illegal?"

"Ha, welcome to Naija! This is life, baby. It's been happening forever."

•

When they pulled into Ondo City, Loladé started to point out all the places of interest. Where Bisi went to school, the house where they'd grown up. Asha cried because her mother couldn't show her this. She cried because her mother spent so long away from it all. She marvelled as its beauty. Blue sky cut against red soil, lush vegetation everywhere. Mango trees were heavy with fruit and flowers that looked like full red lips – *kiss flowers* – were in bloom. In the distance, the magnificent Idanre Mountains with their cloudy peaks took her breath away. The air smelled sweet and people walked slowly – so different to the petrol-gilded atmosphere of Lagos.

They pulled up in front of a house surrounded by a ten-foot wall, with a wrought-iron gate. Kunle got out of the car and hammered a fist against it.

"Tani, eh?" came a voice.

"Emi ni o!" Kunle replied, and after a moment the gates swung open.

Inside Asha and Loladé were greeted by an army of people. Relatives, family friends. They descended en masse, crying, hugging, kissing, welcoming.

The celebration of life lasted ten days. It was a blur for Asha. On the first night an outdoor mass was held, followed by an all-night vigil with a hired band. A goat was slaughtered and people danced, drank and ate until sunrise. Although she'd wanted to bow out early, Asha stayed until 6 a.m. The second day was the funeral. It started with a procession to all the places of significance to her mother – where she was born, primary school, secondary school, houses she lived in. A long line of cars followed behind a band, which followed behind her mother's casket.

The church part was in English and Yoruba and, despite not speaking the native tongue, Asha recognized many of the hymns that her mother used to sing around the house and joined in when she could. After the burial, which Asha couldn't bear to watch, there was a huge party in a field with a large marquee and around a thousand attendees. Area boys provided security. Asha asked Kunle to take her home early.

The morning after the final festivity was Asha's

eighteenth birthday. When she woke up, her first thought was of the red suitcase. She pulled it out from underneath her bed, took the key from where it rested in her handbag, placed the case on her lap and unlocked it. Inside were boxes and letters marked with the names of different family members. Asha found several thick envelopes in mint green, cream, silver and soft pink hues – all addressed to her, with different ages written across the front in gold ink. Her mum had written cards for her 18th, 21st, 25th, 30th and 40th birthdays.

"I wish you were here, Mum," she whispered out loud. She waited a beat, as though her mum might reply, before carefully opening the card meant for today. It was a beautifully delicate handmade card showing the silhouette of a woman with jewel-coloured flowers in her hair, releasing silver and gold butterflies from her palms. Asha ran a hand over the design and then opened it.

Dear Asha,

My darling, my beautiful Shy-Shy Baby! Happy, happy, happy 18th BIRTHDAY! I am so proud of you today!

I cannot thank you enough for the love and care you have shown me over the last few months. I got to see the wonderful woman you are becoming. Believe these words – you have the tools to do amazing things with your life. Your future is destined to be so bright! Your journey from this point is going to be so much fun and such an adventure. Remember that there's a time to be sensible and a time to be carefree. Sometimes you'll make mistakes, fall out with friends and kiss the wrong boys but you will learn from this and grow. And I promise, most of the time, you will constantly find joy in big and small successes. Like getting good grades, graduating, travelling on your own or finally making jollof rice that's as tasty as mine – ha ha!

So here's to your 18th and your first time celebrating in Nigeria. Auntie Loladé will make sure it's one to remember! Eat, drink (not too much!) and be merry.

I love you,

Mama xxxx

Tears rolled down her cheeks but Asha felt truly happy. The kind of happy that you feel in your chest.

The kind that feels like it's glowing outwards from every pore. She clambered across her bed to the window. Throwing the shutters open, Asha stuck her head out, looked up at the clear blue sky and said, "Thank you, Mama. I love you, too!"

A kaleidoscope of butterflies swirled by a tree in the front yard, catching her eye. She watched them, mesmerized. Then her reverie was broken by a loud knocking on her door.

Asha opened it to find several members of her family wearing beaming smiles. They burst into a booming chorus of 'Happy Birthday'.

Loladé snaked her way through to the front of the crowd, grabbed Asha's face in her hands and covered it with a million kisses. "Happy eighteenth, Shy-Shy. We love you!" she said between kisses.

Asha kind of liked the fact that all these people – her new family – had no qualms about coming into her room while she stood there barefoot, wearing pyjama shorts and a T-shirt. She finally understood why her mum had wanted to be buried in Ondo. Her auntie, everyone she'd met, all the places she'd seen, had seemed like a faraway dream when she was younger.

But Asha was connected to every beautiful and chaotic part of it. Nigeria had captured her soul.

A REFUGE

·

Ayisha Malik

"It's not as if one person can change anything," muttered Sabrina, slumping into the back seat of her parents' Toyota.

Her dad was trying to convince her that being here could actually make a difference. She looked at the lights in Calais town centre. With the empty carousel, the setting could work for a bad horror film.

"OK," said her mum to her dad, half laughing. "You know what's coming – left or right?"

"This is our third trip," he replied irritably. "I told you to let me drive."

"No, no. I am *finally* going to find my way."

It was bad enough that Sabrina was missing her friend's birthday party and spending Christmas in a refugee camp, without having to listen to her dad going on and her mum pretending everything was fine. Sabrina sighed and turned up the music on her iPhone. Her old headphones couldn't quite block out their conversation.

"If everyone thought like that, Bee," her dad said, turning round to show he hadn't just ignored her, "we might as well give up now. Change takes time, that's all," he added. "This is going to be good for you, you'll see."

Her dad couldn't even change his tune but he thought he could change the world. Sabrina flicked through her phone. Her parents could've at least bought her some data so she could check her Snapchat and Twitter.

"No! Where are you going?' exclaimed her dad.

He'd been too busy explaining the ways of the world to realize her mum had taken the wrong turn. Sabrina jammed her headphones harder into her ears.

"OK, OK, we're back on track," her mum replied, following the new directions.

"A woman and her sense of direction, eh?" Dad said with a laugh. "Bee?"

She took out a headphone, eyebrows raised.

"If you do one thing in life," he continued, "make sure it's to defy expectations."

Sabrina liked the sound of that – the last thing she wanted was to be predictable. Although she was pretty sure that wasn't what he meant.

"Thank God, we're here," said her mum.

She drove through an open gate and pulled up outside a shoddy warehouse. There were people going in and out, all wearing hi-vis vests, and a group loading up two white vans.

"There's John. Hi!" Her mum got out of the car, jogged up to a tall, lean man and gave him a kiss on the cheek.

"The lifesavers are here," laughed John.

Her dad gave him a brief nod and stood with his hands in his pockets. Sabrina shuffled her feet, hanging back.

"Still here then, John? Perhaps you want to introduce our daughter?" said Dad to Sabrina's mum, whose cheeks flushed.

John's eyes flicked towards Sabrina's mum for a moment before settling on her. He gave a wide smile and strode up to her to shake her hand. "Are you here to work, too?"

Sabrina looked at both of her parents, dug her chin

into her grey knitted scarf and nodded. "Yeah."

John smiled. "And that's why we're winning," he said. "Now, the guys are doing a run with emergency packs and stuff for the women's centre. You know, your mum was a huge help in building that centre."

Her mum waved her hand about, blushing.

"Yeah," added her dad. "Once she actually got here." He laughed and put his arm round her mum.

"What do you want me to do?" asked Sabrina, looking at John.

John stretched out his arm towards the warehouse. "I can show you. Let's begin, shall we?"

•

Her parents went to the camp to help with the emergency packs while John showed her the warehouse. He was constantly hounded by people. *Who moved the shoe section? I've nothing personal against Riffat but she keeps messing up the toy section. Where shall we put things like the hot pants?*

"Hot pants?" Sabrina asked, startled.

"There's nothing a refugee needs more in the winter months," replied John with a wry smile.

"I didn't know people could be that dumb."

He laughed and waved his hand towards a table of jumbled-up clothes, telling her they needed sorting. The other people at the table introduced themselves but once she'd said hello she put in her headphones and switched on her music.

Drake's 'Fake Love' drummed in her ears. She glimpsed people laughing and lowered the volume, almost turning it off when someone smiled at her, but she didn't know how to be a part of this place. She increased the volume again, wishing her headphones worked better.

As the hours wore on, people came and went. They laughed and complained, striding towards shelves and racks, usually either frustrated or focused, and hugged each other a lot – mostly the women. Sabrina eyed them with furrowed brows. What was all this *attachment*? It seemed foreign to her, yet she felt she was missing something she wasn't sure how to reach out for. She changed the track. Gnash sang 'I Hate U, I Love U'. Sabrina kept her eyes on the table.

•

"So? Tell me. How was it?" her mum asked.

They were in their hostel room after dinner, her mum unpacking clothes from the suitcases.

Sabrina shrugged.

Mum paused before adding, "It always takes time to adjust – you might make some new friends."

The wind howled and the rain beat at the window. Sabrina was lying on her bed, flicking through Instagram, Twitter, Snapchat, while her dad was downstairs speaking to a journalist.

"Well, you might make new friends if you ever got off your phone. I wish they didn't have Wi-Fi here."

"What? So I can't keep up with the friends I actually have?" Sabrina retorted, zooming in on a friend's latest selfie. "This place is such a..." *Dump? Waste of time? Both?* "Whatever."

"I suppose we can't all feel the same way about everything," her mum said in a quiet voice as she closed the wardrobe. It didn't shut properly.

Sabrina watched as she inspected the hinges.

Her mum glanced over. "It's a hostel, what do you expect?" she snapped. "We're here to help people who don't even have a roof over their head."

"I never said anything," Sabrina shot back.

Her mum sighed. "Sometimes I wish you would. Instead of expecting us to understand every look you give."

But the only response Sabrina had was a look. She couldn't exactly say: *you and Dad make me this way.* Then her dad walked in. As he closed the door the room seemed to get smaller. He rubbed his hands and blew into them. He was their very own storm of negativity.

"Might as well not have a heater," said Sabrina, putting on another cardigan.

"Maybe you should be telling her about those people in the flimsy tents?" he said, turning to her mum.

Mum paused and looked him in the eye. "You can't teach empathy."

Sabrina did feel bad for the refugees. She really did. But she was too busy watching her mum's face because she knew: you couldn't teach sadness, either.

•

"Fancy doing a run in the van with Steve, Sabrina?" John asked early the next morning when they arrived at the warehouse.

She rubbed her eyes, heavy from lack of sleep, and shrugged. She kept her hands jammed in her coat pockets to stop them from freezing, but at least the sun was out. "I don't mind."

"Good. Your dad's going along, too."

John was distracted by a group of people wheeling a huge trolley into the warehouse, who kept knocking it against a pile of boxes.

"What are you doing?" he shouted to them, making his way towards the mayhem.

She waited with her dad and a few more volunteers as Steve took off his orange hi-vis.

"You won't need these, so just chuck 'em down here. In the jungle it's not 'us' and 'them', yeah? These people are hungry and cold and some of them have been there so long we can't even imagine it. You should be proud cos there are people who don't care and you're here doing something."

Sabrina felt shame mix with the resentment of being made to be here.

"Shall we get to the instructions?" her dad said without looking up, his voice tense.

242

"Sabrina, is it? Yeah, you hand out the jumpers. Nish here'll pass 'em to you while Khalid helps your dad with the line. If things get nasty, everyone get in the van and one of us'll drive."

Sabrina hesitated. "Is it not safe?"

Her dad looked up. "It's not dangerous. But no, it's not safe, either. Have you been listening to Steve? Properly?"

She nodded. She hadn't even checked her phone once.

"After we give out the jumpers," her dad went on, "we can have a look at the rest of the camp." His voice softened. "Just don't wander off on your own, OK?"

His concern reminded Sabrina of the dad she used to know, before all the negativity. When had it begun? Long before her parents started coming to the camp. This charity was supposed to have brought them closer together but it seemed to be doing the opposite.

"All right," she replied.

"Good. Let's go."

•

They drove towards the jungle – her dad in the front with Steve. The rest of them were in the back in complete darkness. When the van stopped it was a few minutes before her dad opened the door, letting in the daylight. They'd only been in there ten minutes, yet the light hurt her eyes.

"Line!" her dad and Steve started shouting.

She got out and looked around at the tents and shelters that stretched as far as her eyes could see. There were groups and groups of people; some sitting around, others hurrying towards the van, where a queue was already forming.

"No pushing."

"What you bring?" Sabrina stared at a teenage boy who'd crept up behind her.

"Jumpers," she replied.

Was she meant to be friendly? Or was she just here to do a job? She took his outstretched hand and shook it.

"Thank you, sister," he said. He smiled. "You give me black hoodie?" he asked.

"Sorry?"

"Keep black hoodie for me, please?"

"Sabrina, stay in the van," came Steve's voice.

Sabrina got back into the van as she watched the boy walk to the back of the line. She was hunched over as one person after another came forwards from the queue, asked for their size and either took it or wanted an exchange.

"Hood. I want black and hood," said a man, his eyebrows knitted in concentration.

Sabrina glanced at the black hoodie she'd set aside for the boy. "Sorry, I don't have one." The man took the jumper she handed to him and moved aside.

"It's because it's the best thing to help them escape at night," explained Nish. "Don't bother with exchanges. Line's getting restless."

Her back was beginning to hurt from hunching when she heard shouting. Khalid seemed to be struggling to keep the queue in order when a hooded boy asked her for a small jumper. When he lifted his head a little, Sabrina saw it was actually a girl who didn't look much younger than herself. A few men pushed forwards so that the line heaved in front.

"I'm sorry," said Sabrina. "You'll have to wait for the women's van."

"But I am cold now." The girl looked at her with big doleful eyes and Sabrina hesitated.

"That's a girl," someone shouted.

"Hurry," she said to Sabrina.

Sabrina hesitated as a scuffle broke out.

"Shut the door," shouted Nish.

Panicking, Sabrina threw the first jumper she saw to the girl – it was the black hoodie. The girl burst into a huge smile.

"*Bee! Bee!*" It was her dad, coming towards her.

But now the girl was staring at her. "You're very pretty," she said.

Before Sabrina knew it, Khalid had got in and shut one of the doors. She caught a glimpse of the boy, looking at the girl with the hoodie that should've been his and shaking his head before Khalid closed the other door, too.

The van started rocking, people banging at the door. Within seconds Sabrina heard the engine start and they made their way back to the warehouse. Her heart thudded as she wondered about the boy she'd kept the hoodie for and the girl who ended up getting it instead.

•

The following day Sabrina found the girl – Homa – again. She was standing around in the same area where they had parked up the day before. Her hands were jammed into a GAP sweatshirt – layered over about five other jumpers.

"Heyyyy, my friend." Homa came over and hugged her.

"Hi," Sabrina said, trying to copy the other girl's ease. "You're not wearing the black hoodie."

Homa put her finger to her lips. "Shh. Boys find out I have it, they will take it from me. They say they have better chance of escaping, but they don't know me."

Homa had a look of mischief but Sabrina thought there was something hard about it, too; resolute.

"Will you? Try to escape?" asked Sabrina. "What about your family?"

"Dead."

Sabrina felt her cheeks flush. "I'm sorry. I shouldn't have asked," she called out.

Because Homa was already climbing on top of a mound and overlooking the jungle as if she were there to conquer it. The cold was biting, but it was a bright day.

Sabrina scrambled up to follow her.

"They died in a bombing a year ago. Me and my

brother come here together. He tried escape one night but fell off lorry. A car hit him."

"Oh, God. I'm so sorry. Did they catch the driver?"

Homa laughed. "Police don't care. They watch while car drives away. How you do your eyeliner like this?"

"Oh," said Sabrina, surprised at how quickly Homa changed the subject. She gave a half shrug. "I'll show you one day."

"Tomorrow?"

Sabrina smiled and nodded.

•

It was Christmas Eve and the past few days Sabrina had gone to the women's centre and spent all her free time with Homa. She'd hardly been on her phone – she knew none of her friends would really get what it was like here. Instead Sabrina taught Homa how to do eyeliner flicks and helped her with her English. Homa in turn showed Sabrina around the camp, introduced her to people and made Sabrina laugh at the impersonations she did of them as soon as they were out of earshot.

"I want to talk like you," said Homa. "Hellooo, how

do you dooo?" she added, putting on a posh English accent.

Sabrina laughed. "I'm not posh. Anyway, your English is already really good."

Homa leaned forwards and said, "When I get to England I will fit in. Just like that. You will help me."

Sabrina felt a knot in her stomach. Homa wasn't made to fit in. She was different in a good way; in a way that Sabrina envied.

They walked towards Homa's tent, past a group of young men. Sabrina looked at the ground as she passed the whistling, feeling her heart beat faster and an anxiety swell in her chest.

"Hey," shouted Homa. "You look at your sister like this?" She'd moved closer to Sabrina and grabbed her hand. Homa turned round, glaring at the men, and spat at the ground.

"Don't," whispered Sabrina. "They'll get angry."

"Good," Homa exclaimed. "Then they'll know how we feel."

They walked the rest of the way in silence.

When they sat down, Homa said, "Do you have a boyfriend?"

"No," replied Sabrina.

"Why?" Homa asked.

Sabrina shrugged. "Do you have one?"

Homa laughed. "You have seen where I sleep?" she exclaimed. "Where would he fit?"

She winked and nudged Sabrina's arm and they both laughed. A gust of wind blew and, as if on cue, the flap of Homa's tent fell off and they both laughed even harder. Inside, Sabrina caught a glimpse of a pile of jumpers, bits of food, a tatty rucksack in the corner.

Homa shot up and closed the flap. "I don't know how many days I'll be here."

At first Sabrina wasn't sure what Homa meant and then she realized she was talking about the jumpers.

"Oh no, I don't… I wasn't…"

But she couldn't exactly say she was horrified at how small it seemed and how, well, *depressing* it was. Even sitting outside the tent she hadn't really absorbed the idea that this was Homa's home right now. Seeing her things in there made everything so … real.

"I'll bring you more," said Sabrina.

"What?"

"Jumpers. Anything. Anything you need."

•

"I just think you should consider how it will be for her when you leave."

Her mum looked at Sabrina over her glass. Another group of volunteers had just walked into the restaurant and her mum's eyes flicked towards the door.

Steve was sitting on the next table, his voice booming. "I've lived through bad shit. I have," he said to the people around him. "But you know what I say to myself?" Steve paused. "I think of Rumi: 'You are not a drop in the ocean. You are the entire ocean in a drop'."

Her dad shook his head. "Could he be any more absurd?"

But the words captured something in Sabrina – they made her feel like she could face the world.

The waiter approached their table.

"It's great that you're doing this but remember that you're not exactly on equal footing," her mum added.

"Bee." Her dad sighed. "Don't be naïve. You should listen to your mum – now and again she'll come out with sense."

She noticed the slight arch of her mum's eyebrow.

"So what? You don't want me to be friends with her?" said Sabrina.

"We brought you here to help people, not make them feel worse than they already do." Her dad sighed again. "The problem is, Bee, you can't save her. She's in for a rough ride. You can help by offering a sympathetic ear and giving her warm clothes—"

"She doesn't want a sympathetic ear. She's not like that."

"This isn't about you. It's—" Her mum paused as the restaurant door opened again, letting in another cold breeze. Sabrina turned round and saw John.

Her mum looked back at the table. "You just have to be careful, that's all."

•

The next day Sabrina packed her rucksack with jumpers, socks and sanitary towels for Homa. Her friends had messaged her about the party and how great it was, and she only felt a slight twinge of regret. Christmas Day wasn't going to be too bad after all – at least she didn't have to spend the whole day with her parents. But when she went into the camp, Homa wasn't at the women's centre like she had promised. Sabrina walked to Homa's tent, the cold wind stinging her eyes.

"Homa? Homa?" She waited. "Homa, it's Sabrina. I've got your stuff."

Giving it another minute or two, she unzipped the flap. Homa was lying down, her back turned to Sabrina. The tent let out a stuffy smell of sweat that mixed with the smell of sewage.

"Homa? Aren't you feeling well?"

It took a few moments before Homa turned round and Sabrina saw she had a black eye.

"Oh my God. What happened?"

Homa gazed at her.

"Homa?" she whispered.

She sat up but winced as she looked at Sabrina's rucksack. "You kept your promise."

"Did someone hurt you?"

"Cowards," Homa said, not meeting her gaze. "They think they know how to shut me up."

Tears of anger fell down Homa's face and Sabrina's throat constricted, her own eyes filling with tears. "What did they...?" She couldn't finish the question.

"No," said Homa. "You don't cry."

"I'm sorry. It's just…"

They were both silent. Sabrina's head buzzed with how quickly things changed. Her parents' voices came into her head: *How will it be for her when you leave?*

What *would* happen when she left? Homa would be all alone. And Sabrina? Had she really cared about a party? And so what if her parents drove her insane? If she went back, knowing what was going on in Homa's world without her, she'd feel alone, too.

"Come with me," said Sabrina, leaning forwards, her voice an urgent whisper.

Homa scoffed.

"We can … we can wrap you up in a cloak or something and fit you in the boot. We'll cover you with all our bags. They won't open the boot. They won't check. I know it."

Her words tumbled out as she barely paused for breath.

Homa looked suspicious. "What about your parents?"

"They're always saying to help people in a way that lasts. They have to do it." She paused and dismissed the idea that they wouldn't help. Because they really did think they could change things – for others if not for themselves. "They have to. When I tell them what happ—"

Homa looked away.

"Sorry. Listen…" Sabrina made Homa look at her. Up close she saw her eye oozed puss. "I promise. You won't have to be alone ever again."

•

She was wrong. Sabrina's dad loomed over her in their hostel room, while her mum seemed to be busy organizing their clothes again.

"It's illegal," said her dad, his hands on his hips. Always asserting himself. "You can't seriously think we'd do such a thing."

"Do you even get what happened to her?" Sabrina's voice broke.

"I'm afraid this kind of thing is quite common," her dad said.

"So that makes it OK?" Sabrina exclaimed.

"That's not what I said. Anyway, your mum and I were having a talk about … things."

She watched her mum take out their suitcase.

"We've decided we're leaving tomorrow."

"What?" She looked at her mum but she'd turned round and started emptying the wardrobes. "Because of Homa? Wait, Mum, stop packing!"

"Some things aren't about you, Bee," said her dad. "Do you want to explain it to her?"

"Please, don't," she replied.

What was happening?

Sabrina's dad strode past her, slamming the door behind him.

"What—"

"Go to sleep, Sabrina."

"But—"

"Just, please. Go to sleep."

That night, as the wind howled, Sabrina thought about Homa in that tent with her bruised face. She turned round in her bed and could see the outline of her mum under her blanket. She was sure she wasn't asleep, either. Her dad's soft snores had been going on for an hour. Did their leaving have something to do with the way her mum looked at John? She felt the urge to get out of bed and put her arm round her. Sabrina stared out of the window and thought about Homa again. Her parents would tell her she had choices: that her life was full of them and yet if Sabrina could choose anything right now, it would be for the people she knew and loved to be safe and happy.

•

"Can I at least say goodbye to her?"

They stood outside the hostel, loading the car with their luggage.

Her dad slammed the boot shut. "For God's sake, Bee."

"Come on, let her," her mum interjected. "I can check up on the centre one last time."

Her dad sighed and then a look crossed his face. "Isn't John doing a delivery there this morning?"

Her mum met his gaze. She almost looked resolute.

"Wouldn't it be lovely to say goodbye to dear old John. Come on, then," he said. "Get in."

She saw her mum close her eyes before climbing into the car.

Sabrina ran, ignoring her mum's shouts. The jungle became a blur, her eyes watered from the cold wind, her nose was running and her legs began to hurt as she sprinted towards Homa's tent, splashing through mud and puddles. But when she called for Homa to come out, there was no answer.

"Homa, hurry! We don't have time."

Finally she unzipped the tent but Homa wasn't there. Everything seemed to look the same – the stack of jumpers, the bits of food, but then she noticed that Homa's rucksack was gone. Maybe she'd gone to the centre. Sabrina ran towards it but no one had seen her there, either. A panic rose up in her. *Was Homa safe? Had something happened to her?*

"Bee," called out her mum. "We're leaving. Come on."

She looked at her mum. This couldn't be it.

"Bee?"

Sabrina shook her head and turned away, running out of the centre and towards the entrance of the camp where she and Homa had first met.

"Homa!" she called out. She ran up to Steve. "Remember that girl?" Sabrina felt herself shaking.

"I got enough volunteers for the run now but you can come with me again later?" said Steve distractedly, looking over her shoulder as he got out his phone.

"What? No, it's … forget it." Sabrina didn't even waste time trying to explain.

She ran back towards the tent but Homa still wasn't there. People were dotted around the place and she recognized one of the men who'd whistled at her – she was sure they were the ones who had hurt Homa. Her chest constricted, her heart thudded. She couldn't look away.

It was when she felt someone walk up next to her that she realized a voice was calling out to her.

"Sister," the voice exclaimed.

It was the boy from the line when she'd first met Homa – the one who'd asked for a black hoodie. Sabrina looked around again but the other man had gone.

Before the boy could speak, she asked him where Homa was.

He smiled. "She run."

"What?" asked Sabrina. "What do you mean?"

"Over fence, past the police." He rubbed his hands together and blew into them, smiling at Sabrina. "You have black hoodie for me now?"

Sabrina started at him for a few moments. "She's gone?"

He nodded, still smiling. "She is tough," said the boy.

Sabrina went into Homa's tent in a daze. Now that she looked closely, she saw the sanitary towels were gone and the pile of jumpers was smaller. A few of the ones she'd given were missing, including the black hoodie. Sitting back, she let the truth sink in. *Homa had actually gone.* Tears surfaced in her eyes. She sat for a while before she brushed them away and walked back to the centre.

•

She saw her parents watching her walk back towards the car.

"Where have you been?" her dad demanded.

Sabrina couldn't say. The question felt too vast.

"Are you OK?" asked her mum.

"I jus—"

"You know, you could teach our daughter some responsibility," her dad interrupted.

Her mum looked at her dad. "Because you're just around for decoration, I suppose?"

Her dad looked like he might say something, then stopped.

"What's the matter?" Her mum's face was close to hers now.

Sabrina felt tears rolling down her cheeks. She shook her head.

"Bee?" She sounded worried.

"She left," Sabrina sobbed. "Homa left."

"Oh, Bee." Her mum bundled her into her arms and let her cry.

"She ran," she said, between sobs.

Why didn't she wait for me?

"Ah. I see," came her dad's voice.

Where in the world was Homa now and where would she end up? Sabrina released herself from her mum's arms and wiped her tears as she saw John, watching them from a distance. He waved at her as both her parents looked at him.

"You'll be back?" he called out.

Her mum smiled – she seemed relieved. Happy. "We'll be back. Come on, Bee," added her mum.

"Will we?" said her dad, looking at her mum.

Her mum went to sit in the driver's seat, car keys in

her hand as she replied, "Yes, we will."

"I'll drive," said her dad.

But her mum ignored him as she sat in the car and put the key in the ignition, and Sabrina got into the back.

"It'll be OK," said her mum, turning round to face her as her dad climbed in the passenger seat, slamming the door.

"I said I'd drive."

Sabrina saw them look at each other – a moment's silence passed between them.

"Say goodbye then, Bee," Sabrina's dad said to her as he looked out of the window.

Sabrina felt an ache in her heart as tears surfaced again. She put in her headphones and switched on Rihanna's 'We Found Love'. Just as Sabrina was about to close her eyes she caught sight of her mum through the rear-view mirror, glancing at her; the flicker of a smile.

"Looks like you know where you're going, finally," her dad commented to her mum.

"Yes. I do."

Sabrina smiled back at her mum. They were on their

way home. As she closed her eyes she realized that if Homa did as she was planning, she'd be making her way to England. Maybe, one day, it would be Homa's home, too.

THE UNWRITTEN FUTURE OF MOSES MOHAMMAD SHABAZZ BANNEKER KING

•

Irfan Master

Moses Mohammad Shabazz Banneker King was brilliant. Not just brilliant in the 'multiplying large numbers to the nearest decimal point'-type brilliant (although he could do that), but brilliant because he could use parts of his brain that others didn't even know existed. Moses was also blind, and had been since he was born, but being named after a prophet, a boxer, an activist, a scientist and a pastor, not being able to see wasn't going to stop Moses changing the world.

This is a story of how he lived. Of how the past collided with the future in a postbox. Of how he bent time to save time. Of how he learned about his present self through his future self.

Moses rarely slept. Sleep was lost time. And time was what he was most obsessed with.

Moses walked the same route to college every day.
And every day he wondered about the heavy brass key
that hung round his neck. He'd had it as long as he
could remember but nobody could tell him how he
had come by it. Raised in foster homes, he had always
thought his mum or dad had put the key round his neck
when he was a baby. Every time Moses felt anxious, he
grabbed at the key and stroked the braille on its stem.
One side: FUTURE. The other: UNWRITTEN.

On the route to college, Moses had various markers
that he could depend on along the way. There was
the bus stop with the crowd of shuffling people, a
road of swaying trees, a man who walked his dog at
exactly the same time every day and always brushed
past him, and lastly, the large square postbox which
told Moses he was almost there. But today, something
was different. Moses had sensed it from a distance.
Approaching slowly, the postbox pulsed with energy.
Stopping in front of it, Moses clutched at his key and
felt a slowing down of time. The quality of the air had
changed, assailing his senses with a strange smell and a
metallic taste in his mouth. His breathing was shallow,
muted so that he could hear the blood rushing in his

ears and a loud pulsing beat, like a heartbeat but from far away. Moses lifted his hand to touch the opening. Locked. The lock on the postbox had the same rough texture as his key. Leaning forwards, Moses tried to listen through the keyhole, but stood up again quickly. He had sensed … everything. All at once. *Everything*.

Moses had been clutching the key in his hand. Pushing the key into the lock and turning, he heard the relentless grating of time. Reaching into the postbox, Moses felt electricity flickering through his body, the hairs on his arm dancing in the air. Then his fingers rested on an envelope covered in braille. He felt initials. The letter was addressed to him, *MK*.

Moses knew this was a letter from the future.

•

Dear Moses,

As-salāmu ʿalaykum.

I thought I'd start with a greeting of peace because the America we live in now is anything but peaceful. And because the speaking of 'other' languages is now prohibited, accept this as my small act of rebellion. My name is Malik. I am writing to you from ~~the~~ A future. I'm eighteen. I am tall. I am clumsy. Some people say I have my father's quick wit, his ~~natural~~ weird intelligence, my mother's ~~way~~ magic with words, but I'm not sure. I'm just me. I'm OK with words. I ~~like~~ love poetry. I write things people want to ~~read~~ feel.

Oh, and sorry about all the crossing out. But some sentences have the right to change ~~their~~ our mind, don't you think? Just like ~~me~~ us.

But why am I writing to you? Well, because you told me to.

OK. I'm not sure ~~how~~ if this is going to work. You promised me it would. Things here are at their worst. Write me back and I'll tell you about our broken future.

Yours expectantly, but confused about the science,
Malik

•

Dear Malik,

Wa'alaykumu salām.

Thank you for your small act of rebellion. I hope

this letter finds its way to you. I'm not sure how but I'm certain that it will – and that means I was right.

If you're writing to me then I've discovered that which has been bubbling in my head since I was thirteen years old. But it also means I must be imprisoned. Or dead... What has happened in your time? Who are you? What is it that you want? Or what is it that I want?

Write back. I must have had a reason for doing what I've done.

Moses

•

Dear Moses,

It worked! Just like you said it ~~might~~ would. You never lied about anything so I shouldn't be surprised, but time-travelling letters – come on!

Serious trouble? Yep. End-times serious.

I have only known this time, but you wrote this note (I added some embellishments) about the day leading up to the spark that started all this.

In exactly seven days time the ~~Dis~~United ~~States~~ Snakes of America will begin to eat its own ~~tail~~ tale. The president will declare a state of emergency and order the National Guard and the army to round up 'illegals' and target those who do not represent the best values of America. Nobody knows what this means. But many call it a war of ~~repatriation~~ exile. There are huge ~~apocalyptic~~ protests on the streets, and violence and dissension within the ranks of the military and National Guard. The forces split into three. A freedom army, an America First army and The Last Army. There is civil war ~~anarchy~~. The borders of Canada and Mexico will close to the US. The flow of trade will ~~slow~~ die. Wall Street will ~~crash~~ burn; people will ~~create~~ enforce segregated communities and defend their patch of land.

You told me to tell you that three years from your time, you will find a theoretical method to create a wormhole. News of your unique research finds its way to the NSA and you disappear when they come for you.

The war breaks out and you and your wife Amal go further underground and that's when you discover it.

What wormholes really are. And how they can be used to traverse time.

I have to go now. It's difficult to write on the move. You told me to tell you that you need to discover now what wormholes are and what needs to be done. We haven't got three years. You have to ~~look~~ see now.

Got to run.

Malik

P.S. I WASN'T BEING FUNNY ABOUT LOOKING NOW!

You'll see. AGAIN NOT BEING FUNNY!

Damn, this cross-future chat is hard.

KEEP YOUR EYE(S) PEELED! (YOU told me to tell you that.)

•

Dear Malik,

I'm married to Amal?! She doesn't even look at me in our thermodynamics class...

Look, I'm only just piecing things together with

my research. I work alone. Nobody at Harvard is taking me seriously. Yet.

I'm just this young blind boy who tells anyone that will listen about the possibilities of wormholes and time travel.

I can't rush this; I still don't know how it works fully. There's a process I have to follow. Physics throws up lots of questions I don't have answers to. And there are rules. I can't bend the rules that exist. And being blind doesn't help. I'm trying to see things through the eyes of those who have never had to rely on others to see. All the research, all the books, all the lectures are by people who can see. I'm just not convinced by them. How they perceive things is totally different to me. I mean, I'm trying to see like them but they're not trying to see like me...

I'm just not there yet. I don't know what to look for. I don't know how I can help.

Sorry.

Moses

●

Moses,

Clearly Amal was ~~waiting~~ hoping for you to make a move... You told me that she always sat just in front of you and waited at the end to open the door for you. Call yourself a brilliant scientist? How much evidence do you need that she might want to talk to you?

I can hear those damned drones overhead. I'd already be dead but they want me alive. That gives me a chance to keep moving. They're closing in. Will keep it short.

I'm a poet not a scientist. I can't help with the physics.

But what I will say is – the thing with seeing is; you don't always have to have your eyes open.

Running now.

Malik

P.S. Re Amal... After five years on the run, you had a child. A boy.

•

Dear Malik,

I have a son! What's his name? This is all too much.
I'll help in any way I can, I just need more time...

What's happened to my family? Are they safe?
My research is unfinished in so many ways and
unwritten in so many others. A lot of the science
is in my head. Knot after knot of argument and
reasoning. Instead of loosening the binds, my mind
just tightens each knot. I need to think...

Write back as soon as you can.

Moses

•

Less than twenty minutes had passed since Moses
had unlocked the postbox, but now time seemed to
accelerate. A minute turned into an hour, an hour into
a day and a day into year. Moses felt rooted to the spot,
the earth spinning on its axis. He sat on the kerb and
waited, braille typewriter discarded beside him. A
letter half-finished caught in the reel. Another letter
explaining that he was close but not close enough

wouldn't help. The postbox still pulsed behind him, a stern reminder that Malik was waiting for a response. In despair and to shut out the world, Moses put his head in his hands.

Being blind from birth meant Moses had found different hues in his darkness. He would never see the glory of an azure sky or the deep tranquillity of an inky black night, but Moses had always lived as if he was stepping carefully through another world. It had always nudged at him, this sense of travelling through another time, another place. He had always heard the roaring sound of water all around him, sometimes to distraction. He went back to that place now, willing it into existence. He walked alone in a landscape with no ground, no sky, no borders, no ending, no beginning. An endless landscape.

He was desperate. His mind was filled with numbers and the impossibility of the problems weighed him down. He had been taught to write proofs for his work, to back it up with research-based evidence. He was constrained by the methods of this world. But sitting upright, Moses realized something. *This world.* He lived in two worlds and, in the other world, the rules were different. His fingers brushed the braille on the key once again and he felt calm.

He had been trying to see how people all around him could see. With their two eyes. But Moses knew he had something else. Something more. He had resorted to looking at the world like those who saw everything in colour and that had always been his problem. He didn't need two eyes or colour to see. He didn't even have to open his eyes. He heard it, then. The regular thump he had thought was blood rushing in his head. It wasn't in his head. It was all around him. Like arteries pumping blood to a heart, he could sense an order to things. And with that realization, Moses smiled and saw with his one eye. The one eye that had always been open.

He knew then what wormholes were, what they were made of and where they went.

His search for the truth wasn't about physics any more, or possibilities or rules. It was about whether he believed what he saw to be true.

Opening his eyes and walking into the heart of what looked like a dark tunnel, Moses Mohammad Shabazz Banneker King could finally see everything.

•

Malik,

Are you there? I saw. I saw what a wormhole is. I saw where they lead and where they all meet. I can see it all but I still don't know what I can do to change the future. I can't see the future. Yet.

Who are you? Why did I choose you?

Moses

•

Moses,

We haven't much time.

You told me to be patient with you but I'm so tired... Tired of running. Tired of waiting. I still don't know if we can change this future but you were convinced... I ~~could~~ should have gone with you...

We have one chance to change the ~~future~~ past.

The president spent a part of his childhood in Iran. Son of a three-star general turned diplomat. His mother died when he was just a little boy and his Iranian nanny raised him. Her name is Shireen. The president called her mother.

You told me that you saw this with your eye. That this was the only way and this, the only moment we would have. You were convinced that we could use her... Find her and this could all end.

I'll see you.

Malik

•

Shireen Hafizi covered her head with her scarf and stepped out into the busy Queens street. She rarely left her small apartment these days; scared she'd be rounded up and taken to the camps like so many people she'd known. Disappeared. Today was the day the president was coming to town to sign a special decree and Shireen was determined to see him, even if he couldn't see her. Once upon a time, he had been just a boy. John. Her boy. She thought back to when his father told John that he was to be posted back to America, he had grabbed her leg and sworn that he .

wouldn't leave without her.

Shireen had loved him with all her heart. Singing Farsi lullabies to him, holding him when his father admonished him for crying and recounting stories from the *Shahnameh* for him to marvel at. She saw him leave home and become something else, pursuing the political destiny laid out for him before he was born. He had become hard, difficult, resolute in his convictions. He had forgotten her and the world she had shown him. No longer the gentle boy she had loved. And now he was coming to New York to sign one of the most important documents in US history. And she wanted to see him one more time.

The crowds were already gathering. Shireen could feel an overwhelming anger pulsing all around her. After today, the world she knew would be on its knees.

The National Guard was already on the street. Shireen shuffled as close as she could to the front of the barrier outside the UN building and waited. He arrived as part of a long convoy of cars and stepped out. The crowd was already pushing against her and she almost fell. She craned her neck to see him, just as the crowd exploded. The barricade broke and she was shoved to the ground as police and armed guards raced to intercept the protesters. She felt a hand gently lift her to her feet. A young boy, with a stick and dark glasses.

"Come with me. I'll take you to him."

"Who are you?" Shireen asked the boy.

"I'm Moses."

"What are you doing here?"

"I'm trying to change the future."

Shireen shook her head. "Nobody can change what is written."

Shireen looked at the chaos all around her and the calm way the young boy held himself. He was clearly blind, but the way he stared at her suggested he could see her somehow. That he knew her story. Taking his hand, Shireen followed the boy as he made his way through the crowd. As he led her away, his stick created an aura around them and not a single person got close enough to touch. They entered the UN building through a door at the back, unnoticed.

Moses led Shireen down a corridor and stopped in front of some lift doors. Producing his key, Moses felt for a keyhole and turned. The doors opened and

Shireen took a step back, sensing a great vastness.

"He'll come this way."

"How do you know?"

"I just do."

"What will I say to him?"

"That's up to you."

"I love him like a son but I can't change his mind…"

"No, nobody can."

"What can I do?"

Looking right at her, Moses took her hand and spoke gently in hushed tones.

Shireen stood rigid with shock. "Is this the only way?

"It gives us time to try and find another way."

Adjusting her scarf, Shireen regained her composure. Nodding in agreement, she turned to Moses.

"And you? Will you find your way?"

"I'll find a way," said Moses, and shuffled into a recessed part of the corridor.

From the left came the president, flanked by secret-service agents.

He saw Shireen and froze in recognition. "*Maman*? What are you doing here?"

"I came to see my son."

"You shouldn't be here."

"Who has the power to say who should be here or not? I left my homeland to be here. To be with you."

"Maman … it's more complicated than that… I have to sign this decree to secure my country."

"Our country, my child, it's my country, too."

"I wish it was so easy. Our future is at stake."

Shireen stepped forwards, speaking in Farsi to soothe him.

She turned to Moses and nodded.

The president looked over Shireen's shoulder and saw Moses. Gently taking the president's hand, Shireen led him into the lift. A secret-service agent moved to step in behind them but the president held up his hand.

"It's OK. I'm safe with her. She used to look after me." The secret-service agent tried to interrupt him but the president had already pressed the button in the lift.

Moses heard the doors close and the lift ascend. Breathing deep, he slowed time. By the time the lift reached the top floor, the world would have spun on its axis once more. When Moses had explained to Shireen, simply yet directly, what would happen after they entered the lift, she had been horrified. There really was no good way to explain the unpredictable nature of being lost in time.

In the days to follow, there would be many stories about the president's disappearance. The official White House statement would claim the president had had a massive heart attack and died. Arrangements for a state funeral were already under way. The nation was in shock and in the aftermath, the anger that had built for years was diffused. The protestors, tired and beaten, went home. The National Guard disbanded and the army stood down. A new future had been written.

Throwing his guiding stick into a bin, Moses used his key to open another door into the darkness and stepped through.

•

Moses,

We did it! We changed everything!

It's like watching the world from behind a waterfall. I'm just waiting to step through. But you told me to wait, so here I am.

I'm sorry I didn't tell you who I was but you told me, no matter what, that I wasn't to say.

I'm your son. Malik Mohammad Shabazz Banneker King.

Before you left, you gave me detailed instructions. I was not to listen or be distracted by anything you had to say. Under normal circumstances that would have been great, but it was a bit stressful, if I'm honest.

And then there's the other thing. The hardest part.

You made me swear not to say anything. About Mum. I was fifteen when they captured her and took her to an internment camp. They knew she was your wife. That they could get close to you through her. She … she wouldn't let that happen and…

I'm so sorry, Dad. She died in that place.

That's why you left. Why I'm still here.

You managed to change the future but you left to find a past where she doesn't die.

Dad, I need ~~love~~ you. I don't want to be here by myself. We changed the future but without you, I'm ~~losing~~ gaining time.

I'm going to take the same path you took. The only one I know is open.

You've gone looking for Mum. I'm coming looking for you.

Your son in this time and the next,
Malik

•

There ends a story of how the past collided with the future in a postbox. How time could be bent but not broken. How one eye was better than two eyes. How one man goes looking for his love but ends up losing his heart. How this story ends in this time, but is only just beginning in another place.

FORTUNE FAVOURS THE BOLD

·

Yasmin Rahman

TERRORIST ATTACK IN NIGHTCLUB

With a quivering thumb, I click on the headline. The website takes an infinity to load and I can feel my heart pounding faster, faster, faster, hear the mantra echoing in my head: *Please don't be another Muslim. Please. Please. Please. Not again.*

The article finally fills my screen. My eyes are immediately drawn to the photograph of a street aglow with blue lights. An ambulance with its doors wide open waits for an oncoming stretcher; it's pretty dark, but you can still see the blood pooling out of the patient's chest.

A mass shooting took place at Mischief nightclub at 3.15 a.m. this morning. So far, seven people have been confirmed dead, including the gunman, who was killed by the police. Eleven others are in a critical condition.

"Looking at porn again?" Nims laughs, dropping on to the bed next to me and snatching the phone out of my hand. The bed dips so that we bump into each other, but the warmth from her body does little to stop the chills exploding all over my skin.

"Oh great, another one?" Nims asks after a second. She doesn't even bother reading the whole article, just throws the phone into my lap and stands up. I grab it back and read the words as quickly as my eyes can scan them.

Pakistani immigrant. Heard shouting in Arabic. Islamic State.

I click on article after article, each telling a slightly different version of events: one says he singled out women, while another says he closed his eyes and shot at random. But the thing they're all sure about is his religious motivation.

"Stop it already," Nims says, snatching the phone from me again.

She's already changed into her uniform while I'm sitting on the bed, still in my dressing gown. Her eyes are soft and unaffected, her head tilted slightly to the left. There's a lot of things about Nims that I'm jealous of. Her ability to not give a crap is one of them.

"Just … *don't*, OK? Don't think about it," she says, squeezing my shoulder.

Because it's that easy.

Well, I guess it really is for her – she doesn't have a stupid brain that's wired all wrong.

I just nod and stand up on my jelly legs.

Seven confirmed dead, eleven others in a critical condition.

•

Granny is the only one awake when we get downstairs. She's sitting in her usual seat by the fireplace, scribbling furiously in the colouring book in her lap as the TV flickers in front of her. Nims walks straight into the kitchen but my eyes are immediately drawn to the TV screen. Police cars line the street, forensics in their white suits walk in and out of the building, people stand around hugging.

"Morning," Granny says, not even looking up.

I grunt in response, watching the news banner scroll across the bottom of the screen.

Islamic State have taken responsibility for this attack

in a video message posted online. Suspect has been named as—

The screen snaps to black.

"Hey, I was watching that," Granny chides, her eyes finally detaching from the paper.

"Oh, really?" Nims asks, suddenly right beside me with the remote in her hand. "Cos it looks to me like you were drawing in a kid's book."

"It's called mindfulness!" Granny rebuts, brandishing her orange pencil at Nims. "You should try it sometime, it'll make you less angry."

"Seems to be working wonders on you."

They have their signature stare-off and, as usual, it ends with Granny just shaking her head and muttering under her breath in Bengali.

"Your cardboard's getting cold," Nims says, taking my hand and pulling me into the kitchen where she's laid out our breakfast: a piece of buttered toast for me and cold leftover Chinese food for her.

I sit down and start picking off chunks of the crust.

Seven confirmed dead.

Eleven others in a critical condition.

Pakistani immigrant.

Islamic State.

"Zaibah!" Nims waves her hand in front of my face until my eyes unfocus from the plate. "Are you even listening?"

"Huh?" I blink a few times and find my breakfast reduced to a pile of torn-up chunks. "What did you say?" I pop a piece of toast into my mouth. It really does taste like cardboard today.

Nims just stares, one eyebrow raised slightly, the fork now sticking out between her closed lips. After a second she straightens her posture and starts twirling some more of the noodles on her plate. No matter how many times I tell her cold leftovers for breakfast is both gross and inappropriate, she refuses to listen. She's never been one to follow the rules.

"Wanna Freaky Friday today?" she asks with a smirk that manages to crack me.

"Yeah, cause that's gonna work," I chuckle.

The last time we did a Freaky Friday was in Year Nine, when Nims had a maths test she hadn't bothered to study for. Despite the pencil slipping from my hand multiple times, I managed to finish the test, pretty confident I'd done well. When Mrs Honley came round collecting our papers, I lowered my head and hid behind my curtain of hair (I'd worn it down, just like Nims always does). As soon as the bell rang, I started shoving everything into my bag, desperate to go and find Nims and collect my reward of Reese's Peanut Butter Cups (Nims always preferred money). I was just about to stand up when Mrs Honley's voice boomed over all the clattering chairs.

"Class, let's all take a second to thank Zaibah for joining us today. I do hope she learned something."

Everyone turned to look at me, the laughs starting as a roar instead of a whisper. My face burned and I tried to hide it with hair again.

"Tell Nilima we missed her," Mrs Honley said as I sank further down in my chair. "And that she'll be taking this test in detention tomorrow."

It was easier to do stuff like that back then, before I started wearing a headscarf, when we were truly identical. I've never regretted my decision but I do wonder what it would be like if I'd listened to Nims and waited until college, where people are apparently 'less likely to be twats'.

"Well, the offer's there," Nims says. "Might even be

fun." She scrapes the plate with her fork, scooping up the last of her food.

I can't say I'm not tempted to swap. I know it won't completely change things, that I'll still feel like everyone's looking at me when I walk down the corridors, desperate for me to show that I know about the shooting, for me to prove that I don't condone it, that we're not all like that. But maybe it would ease my mind a bit. Things have always been different at school for Nims, even before I separated myself with my headscarf. There's just something about her that screams 'don't mess with me'. I sometimes try to mirror her movements, her facial expressions, the way she talks to others, but I'll never be like her.

"Better yet," Nims continues in her trademark mischievous tone, "we could just skip altogether. Go into town, spend some of that Eid money you've got saved up." She pushes back her chair and walks to the sink to dump her plate.

"I already told you," I scold, slipping the rest of my toast into the bin and saying a little prayer in my head for wasting the food. "I'm not buying you those shoes."

"You wouldn't be buying them for me, you'd be

buying them for *us!*" She grins.

I just roll my eyes at her. She rummages through the takeaway containers on the counter and pulls out a couple of fortune cookies.

"Catch," she says to me, half a second before launching the cookie at my face. I'm used to her antics though and I manage to catch it by the tips of my fingers. Nims laughs as she cracks hers open. "*If you have something good in your life, don't let it go,*" she reads.

Before I can even unravel mine, she jumps over and wraps her arms round me.

"You're hurting me," I laugh. "Get off!"

"Nuh-uh," she says, squeezing harder. "Fortune cookie told me not to."

I try to wriggle away. "I need to do the dishes!"

"Later, later. Read your fortune first."

Her grip finally loosens and I step back out of her reach, unfurling the little piece of paper.

A chance encounter could open new doors to healthy change and friendship. Remember, fortune favours the bold.

•

When I return to the living room, Granny has started watching one of her awful Bollywood films, the pencil hanging limp in her hand. Nims sits on the other end of the sofa, tapping away on her phone, but I can tell she's really watching the TV, too. The remote lies abandoned on the table. My brain begs me to flip back to the news channel – to get an update, to gather as much information as I can to defend myself later on, but I force myself to resist.

"C'mon, let's go," I say, rushing to the front door and putting on my shoes. Nims follows lazily.

"Say *Ayatul Kursi* before you leave!" Granny shouts as I shoot out of the door, leaving Nims with one shoe in her hand.

•

Nims giggles on the phone to Noah the whole way to the bus stop. I walk five steps behind to give them privacy but inside I'm begging her to hang up. I need her chatter directed towards me, to distract me, to make me forget the headlines, the images of bloody bodies being wheeled out. There's just something about Nims that has a calming effect; it's one of the many ways she's the better twin.

A woman in a suit walks towards us, eyes glued to her phone. Her cute little puppy begins skipping and barking when it sees me. Nims always jokes that I'm a sixteen-year-old Dr Doolittle. I'll admit it *is* kinda eerie how animals are instantly attracted to me. I crouch down as the poodle yaps at my ankles, the bell on her pink collar tinkling. There's a spot just behind the ears that dogs love and this cutie is no different, she emits a contented sigh as my fingers work their magic.

"Who's a good girl?" I laugh as she wags her tail like crazy.

The puppy raises her front paws on to my knees, pushing her head further into my hand.

"Oh, you're absolutely adorable, you are," I tell her. She seems to understand because she licks my hand.

"Poppy!" the suit woman shouts from a few metres away.

The dog whines once as I look up at the woman. I usually love talking to people about their pets but I can immediately tell from the furrowed eyebrows and downturned mouth that this woman is in no mood for a conversation.

"Sorry," I say to her, standing up as the dog pads back. "I was just—"

"Poppy, come," the woman says, actively avoiding eye contact with me.

I tug on my scarf, making sure it's fixed in place as the woman jerks the lead so the puppy whimpers on its way back.

"Sorry," I repeat. Apologizing is my go-to defence mechanism in these situations. I expect her to give an excuse, that she's in a rush or something, but she doesn't even look my way. I wave to the puppy as she's dragged away, inwardly cursing her owner. People like that don't deserve pets.

As the woman walks away, I pull out my phone to make it seem like I'm unaffected if she does decide to turn round. But before I know it, I'm back on the internet, scanning for any new information. A 'Breaking News' alert pops up but as I click on it, I bump into Nims's back and almost drop my phone.

"Oh crap," I groan, rubbing my forehead. "Why'd you stop?"

"That's kinda the point of a bus *stop*," she laughs, pulling up her bag strap.

I try to think of a witty response, but settle for a lame, "Oh."

Nims laughs. "Who're you texting, anyway?"

"Maybe you're not the only one with a secret boyfriend," I tease, slipping the phone back into my pocket. There's no point telling her the truth. Nims doesn't understand my anxiety – she's probably already forgotten about the news, probably won't even think about it again for the rest of the day.

"Speeeaaaking of which," she says slowly.

I stare at her. She bites her lip, which means she wants something. No prizes for guessing what.

"You're ditching me *again*?"

"Not *ditching*. It's just … Noah's brother got a new car – it's like *super* fast. He's gonna drop us to school." She pauses for a fraction of a second. "You can totally come with us. I'm sure—"

"Uh, no thanks," I say, my fingers clenching around my bag strap. This is the third time this week she's ditched me for Noah.

"Do you mind?" she asks softly, cocking her head and

fluttering her eyelids, like she always does. Despite my annoyance, the sight makes me smile.

I roll my eyes at her. "You're a terrible sister."

Her smile reaches breaking point as she squeezes my arm and says, "Only because you're the best one ever."

She kisses my cheek and begins to walk away but then quickly swivels back round as I perch on the seat in the bus shelter, taking out my phone to load up the latest episode of the *Dear Hank and John* podcast. I want her to say she's changed her mind, for her to choose me over Noah.

"Oh, wait," she says instead, rummaging through her bag. "You'll probably need this."

I laugh a little when she pulls out an inch-wide plastic cube covered in a variety of different surfaces.

"When did *you* get a fidget cube?" I ask as my fingers eagerly explore the anxiety aid. I press a few of the rubber buttons then roll the little joystick round a few times before landing on my favourite, the light switch. The clicks never fail to calm me down.

Nims shrugs. "Thought it'd come in handy since you *always* forget yours."

I take a deep breath, the cube already working its magic. "Thanks."

•

The bus pulls up a few minutes later. I take out my headphones and psyche myself up by letting everyone else on first but it's still terrifying stepping on and flashing my card at the uninterested driver. I feel the atmosphere change right away. Eyes move towards me. Conversations stop. Whispers start.

Seven confirmed dead.

Eleven others in a critical condition.

Pakistani immigrant.

Islamic State.

I notice a group of Year Seven boys who aren't usually on this bus sitting in the front row on both sides. I dip my head and walk up the aisle, clicking the light switch on the fidget cube furiously.

"Oi, oi," one of the boys says in a delighted tone.

I instinctively look up.

"All right, raghead?" number two says.

"Nah, bruv, she probably don't speak English, ya know?"

They cackle.

"Can I get past, please?" I mumble, looking down at the pile of their backpacks that are obstructing my path.

"Sorry, I don't speak Muslamic," number four says.

They cackle again.

I want to disappear. Just completely disintegrate into thin air. If the bus wasn't already moving, I'd turn round and get off. Even being a third wheel to Nims and Noah is better than this. I look around, hoping that someone else on the bus will stick up for me but everyone looks away.

I grab on to one of the poles to steady myself and stretch my leg as far as possible to step over their bags without touching them. I make my way towards the back of the bus. I'm scared that the boys are going to follow me … or worse, follow me round school all day, or that they're going to be on this bus every day from now on. I begin to recite *Ayatul Kursi* in my head, hoping the prayer for protection will kick in before things get worse. My heart's pounding as I pass an old woman with a million bags sitting in an aisle seat. Our eyes connect for a brief moment before she awkwardly looks away, clutching her purse tight to her chest.

The boys are still hollering when I get to a free seat at the back. I plop down and shove in my headphones, fumbling to start up the podcast again, pushing the volume to the highest limit. I make the mistake of looking up. One of the boys opens his mouth as we lock eyes, but I snap my head back down and focus my attention on the fidget cube again, inspecting the ridges of the tiny gears as I spin them, the sharp plastic digging into my fingertips.

I imagine Nims riding in Noah's brother's car, sticking her head out into the wind as they speed down the road. I turn towards the window, hoping to see her. But even the version of her in my imagination disappoints me. I pull myself away from these thoughts and try to lose myself in the podcast.

It takes a few minutes but I feel myself relax a bit just as Hank and John begin their signature sign-offs. The boys are still at the front but now they're too busy flicking their fingers about trying to make the clicky noise to pay any attention to me. Apparently *Ayatul Kursi* really does work.

The bus slows to a stop in front of Asda as the

podcast comes to an end. As I flick through my phone for something new, I hear the boys start to holler again. My head jerks up, face already burning, the headphones popping out of my ears. I expect the idiots to be pointing at me and laughing but instead their mockery is aimed towards a girl who's standing to the side to let a group of people off the bus.

"Oi, oi. 'Ere's another one, boys."

"All right, raghead?"

Instead of cowering and running away like I did, this girl turns to face the boys head-on. I recognize her right away – she's one of the few other people who wears a headscarf at school. I don't even know her name but I find myself watching her on campus sometimes. I think she's in Year Eleven.

"Can I help you?" she asks calmly.

The boys snigger, nudging the leader of the pack who sits in an aisle seat. The bus begins to move again but the girl doesn't even need to hold the pole to remain upright.

"Yeah, yeah," the leader says, standing up. His shirt is untucked, the collar upturned. His blue and gold tie hangs undone round his neck. "We was jus' wondering why you lot like killing people so much. Like, that's what you're told to do, right? Kill peeps?"

"Yeah," number four pipes up. "Like, that shooter. Was he like your brother or something?"

The others snicker, waiting for the girl to break down.

But she doesn't.

She doesn't run down the aisle, fighting back tears, digging her nails into her palms like I would. Like I did.

"Are you really stupid enough to believe that all Muslims are related?" the girl asks. "There's over a billion of us, you know."

The leader is momentarily shocked but he recovers quickly. "You're all the same though, innit? All Paki terrorists."

"Great mentality you've got there," the girl says in a semi-bored tone. "Your parents must be so proud."

"No, right," he says. "It's facts, innit. Terrorists are *always* Muslims."

"Well, I can't really argue with facts, can I?" the girl muses. "But if we're going with statistics, then you four must all be rapists, right? Or future paedophiles?

Since they're *always* white males."

The boys are silent. I'm holding my breath. The old woman with the millions of bags stares at the girl. I swear even the bus radio goes silent.

"Nah, nah, like..." number three starts up. "You Pakis—"

The girl cuts him off. "Let me know when you learn to speak English and we can continue this conversation, yeah?" she says like a badass.

She holds her head up high as she walks away, like actors do in action movies as a car explodes behind them. She kicks their bags aside to get past. Our eyes lock for a second and I realize I'm staring with my mouth slightly open. I quickly shut it and blink a few times. She smiles at me as she sits down a few rows in front. The boys look at each other for a second before feeling confident enough to start up again.

"Yeah, you better run!" one of the boys shouts towards her.

"Oh, just be quiet," one of the other passengers *finally* says.

The boys all just look at their trainers, muttering among themselves. The leader sits down. I can't help but stare at the girl... Well, the back of her head, anyway. Her scarf is wrapped in the same style as mine, her shade of blue just a few notches lighter. There's nothing obviously remarkable about her and yet somehow I'm in awe. I always thought Nims was the epitome of confidence, the person I should aspire to be, but this girl just completely blew her out of the water. Even Nims wouldn't have dealt with that as well as she did.

As I watch the girl sitting in her seat, her head up, facing straight ahead, daring someone to mess with her, I can't help but think of my fortune from the cookie earlier.

A chance encounter could open new doors to healthy change and friendship. Remember, fortune favours the bold.

I find myself grabbing my bag and standing up. I feel like everyone's gaze is on me. My instinct is to duck my head, to avert my eyes, to draw as little attention to myself as possible, but then I remember the girl's sense of poise. I channel her confidence as I walk down the aisle towards her.

"Um, hi," I say, forcing myself to make eye contact

with her. "Can I… Do you mind if I…?"

The girl looks up at me, confused, but there's still a slight smile on her face. There's no indication that the encounter with the boys even happened.

"Can I sit here?" I finally manage to ask.

"Of course!" she says, without a moment's hesitation. She pulls her bag on to her lap and moves across to the seat near the window.

"I'm Mariam," she says, extending her hand.

I take a second to look from her hand to her face, every bit of her seems to be the person I wish I was, the person I want to be. Her confidence is piercing – it's strange to be looked at so intently, to be *seen*.

"I'm Zaibah," I say, shaking her hand.

OF LIZARD SKIN
AND DUST STORMS

·

Inua Ellams

of all the things I left behind
of fresh suya and fura de nunu
of harmattan winds and dust-thick evenings
of cattle pastures and dried bush meat
of sand-dune sunsets and ever-warm springs
of Muslim fathers and Christian mothers
of Christmas hymns and Eid al-Fitrs
of morning prayers and exercise books
of first days and nursery schools
of goat's milk and mathematics
of plantains and punctuation
of low angles and hanging fruit
of catapults and mango trees
of swollen stomachs and sticky fingers
of sick beds and feasting mosquitoes
of malaria and chloroquine
of soaked roots and boiled leaves
of old ways and remedies
of flickering lightbulbs and empty generators
of plunging nights and soupy darkness
of hurricane lamps and shadow play
of folk stories and firelight
of wild imaginations and feverish delight

of delirium and sweat-drenched slumber
of ancestral belonging and deep lineage
of wet earth and open wombs
of warm swamps and slow silence
of twilight and quiet songs
of rebirth and easy breeze
of gentle dawns and strengthening fists
of bright worlds and parched tongues
of sunlight and flowing curtains
of boredom and twitching fingers
of catapults and new fruits
of all the lessons I never learned
of the child of chaos I once was
of the man I've become.

About the Authors

Mary Florence Bello was born in north London to Nigerian parents and grew up on a diet of tales from Yoruba culture. She studied law and worked in finance before embarking on a career as a journalist.

Aisha Bushby was born in the Middle East. After spending some time in Kuwait, Lincolnshire, Birmingham, Vancouver and Cheltenham, she now lives in Cambridgeshire and is working on a YA novel.

Tanya Byrne was born in London and now lives in Brighton. Her mother was Guyanese and her father was Irish. She left BBC Radio to write her debut novel, *Heart-Shaped Bruise*. Since then, she has also written *Follow Me Down* and *For Holly*.

Inua Ellams was born in Nigeria and now lives in London. He is an award-winning poet, playwright, performer, graphic artist and designer. He has published three pamphlets of poetry and his first play, *The 14th Tale*, was awarded a Fringe First at the Edinburgh International Theatre Festival.

Catherine Johnson was born in London. Her dad was from Jamaica and her mum was Welsh. Her books include the YA Book Prize-shortlisted *The Curious Tale of Lady Caraboo*, and *Sawbones*, which won Young Quills best historical novel. She also writes for film and TV, including *Bullet Boy*.

Patrice Lawrence was born in Brighton and brought up in an Italian-Trinidadian household in mid Sussex. She now lives in east London. Her first novel, *Orangeboy*, was winner of the Waterstones Children's Book Prize for Older Children and the YA Book Prize, and shortlisted for the Costa Children's Book Award.

Ayisha Malik is a British Muslim born and raised in south London. She has spent various spells teaching, being a book publicist and editor. Her debut novel, *Sofia Khan Is Not Obliged*, was met with great critical acclaim. She has also ghost-written *The Secret Lives of the Amir Sisters* with Great British Bake Off winner Nadiya Hussain.

Irfan Master was born in Leicester to an Indian father and Pakistani mother. His debut novel, *A Beautiful Lie,* was shortlisted for the Waterstones Children's Book Prize and the Branford Boase Award. He has worked as a librarian and a project manager at the National Literacy Trust, before becoming a full-time writer.

Musa Okwonga was born in London to Ugandan parents and is now based in Berlin. He is a journalist, musician and the author of two books about football, a poetry collection, *Eating Roses for Dinner*, which J.K. Rowling described as brilliant, and a contributor to *The Good Immigrant*.

Yasmin Rahman is a British Muslim born and raised in Hertfordshire. She is currently working on her second MA, in Writing for Young People at Bath Spa University. She co-founded and edits online literary magazine *Scrittura* and creates fan art for her favourite books.

Phoebe Roy is part Indian and part Jewish, and is from north London. She has a first-class degree and master's in Archaeology and Ancient History. She has worked as an editor, tutor, production editor, ghost writer and features writer.

Photo © Shampat Productions

Nikesh Shukla is a British Indian Londoner, now living in Bristol. He is author of Costa First Novel Award-shortlisted *Coconut Unlimited*, and *Meatspace*, and editor of *The Good Immigrant*, winner of the Books Are My Bag Readers' Choice Award and for which he was named in *Foreign Policy* magazine's 100 Global Thinkers of 2016.

About the Illustrator

Lucy Banaji is part English, part Indian and grew up in south-west London. She trained in fine art and is a self-taught illustrator. Lucy has worked in various areas of illustration including publishing, stationery and website rebranding. She creates bold and fun illustrations by combining both handmade and digital textures.

Topics and Resources

Bereavement
The protagonist in 'Dear Asha' (p.197) is coming to terms with the loss of her mother. Cruse Bereavement Care (www.cruse.org.uk) offers help, advice and information.

Islamophobia
Islamophobia is dealt with in 'Fortune Favours the Bold' (p.289). Tell MAMA UK (www.tellmamauk.org) is a secure and reliable service for reporting anti-Muslim abuse.

Obsessive Compulsive Disorder
The protagonist in 'Marionette Girl' (p.19) has OCD and her behaviours are explicitly outlined in the story. OCD UK (www.ocduk.org) supports those affected by Obsessive Compulsive Disorder.

Racism
The protagonist in 'We Who?' (p.121) encounters racist and fascist viewpoints. Organisations such as Hope Not Hate (www.hopenothate.org.uk) offer anti-racism resources and advice.

Refugees
The protagonist in 'A Refuge' (p.232) volunteers at a refugee camp. Unicef (www.unicef.org.uk) supports refugee children across Europe.

Sexuality
The protagonist in 'Hackney Moon' (p.83) is part of the LGBTQ* community. Stonewall (www.stonewall.org.uk) provides support and advice on LGBTQ* issues.

Terrorism
In 'Fortune Favours the Bold' (p.289) a terrorist attack at a nightclub is reported. Childline (www.childline.org.uk) have resources covering terrorism and its ramifications.

Acknowledgements

Stripes would like to thank Julia Kingsford and Sarah Shaffi for their insightful input into selecting the four new voices included in this anthology, Aa'Ishah Hawton for becoming an invaluable member of the #ChangeBook team as our editorial mentee, and everyone who has shown their support for the project – we've been overwhelmed by the response before the book has even been published.